SIMON PETRIE

I HAVE NO LEGS
AND I MUST MANSPREAD

Typeset in Dolly Pro / Candara
Cover illustration by James Morrison, derived from an image by Karsten Winegeart on Unsplash

National Library of Australia Cataloguing-in-Publication entry:

Title: I Have No Legs And I Must Manspread / Simon Petrie.
ISBN: 9780648383680 (pbk.)
Subjects: Science fiction, Australian.
           Short stories, Australian.
Dewey Number: A823.4

TABLE OF CONTENTS

Also by this author

(the Titan sequence)

Matters Arising from the Identification of the Body

Wide Brown Land

Soft Dim Skies

A Reppraisal of the Circumstances Resulting in Death (forthcoming in 2026)

(not the Titan sequence)

Flight 404

Murder on the Zenith Express: the Gordon Mamon collection

80,000 Totally Secure Passwords That No Hacker Would Ever Guess

The 1001 Top Immortality Treatments You Must Try Before You Die

Tremendously Inconveniencing A Great Many Photons

Wayfaring Stranger

Not by this author

Pointy Enders (by a different Simon Petrie)

Also not by this author

The Photon of the Opera

Trepanation Without Trepidation

Manifestations of Chromatic Regularity in the Terrestrial Urban Traffic Light

Jane's All The World's Non Sequiturs

For those who love science,

good trouble,

and the ways which do not harm

INTRODUCTION/AUTOFICTION

If there was a deathmatch, somehow, between the four horsemen of the apocalypse and the five stages of grief, who would win?

Well, the five stages of grief, obviously, because they're real.

But let's say it was a battle royale, continuing until only one combatant survived, who would that be? Bargaining, depression, acceptance, they have their place but they'd be useless in a fight. It'd come down, ultimately, to anger brawling with denial. Anger would start strong but would burn itself out too quickly. Look around. Denial's the one with staying power. You know I'm right.

There'll come a time when the author's not there. I find myself wondering what that will be like, partly for myself but also for the books, but obviously I can't know, that's just part of the one-sided and frankly rather stupid deal which we have with entropy. Now I intend to be around for a good while yet, but it's a sad fact that this situation of not being here gets one book closer with each book completed, and one seldom knows in advance, unless a wing falls off at eleven kilometres up or some such. My usual way of dealing with this eventual self-absence is through denial, the victor in the scenario outlined above, but it must be said that my mind has been more on mortality, both my own and others', these last few months.

In April I flew back to New Zealand at short notice with my son, to see my father one last time. Dad was and was not in a room at the funeral home in Rangiora; the next day, he was and was not buried in the rural churchyard cemetery just a few kilometres from the farm where he grew up, the farm where he died. The farm is a place where I still belong, and yet I can never stay for long; that's how it is. I've wondered, since, what my dad, a second son who stayed doggedly with farming, made of me, a second son who didn't; we never talked of such differences, and maybe that too is denial, in a sense. I'll miss him: an old man who didn't actively try to make the world worse, at a time (gestures wildly at *all this*) when so many of them do. I'll miss the knowledge that my old pairs of shoes, discarded at the end of each visit, would fit him, the biosecurity-declaration shortcut for the airport on the way back: yes, I've been overseas, on a farm, but not with these shoes. It's always quicker than nothing to declare. I'll still leave the shoes, next time, but there's less value in doing so: my brother's feet are larger, so he can't use them.

But this is a book you hold, of several strange little stories, and it's the author's hope that these stories will benefit the reader in some small way. If they do, and if it happens that you're reading or re-reading these words in the decades hence, when the author is no longer anywhere, then it's the author's wish that you should raise a middle finger in his memory, against that frankly rather stupid deal which we have with entropy, and against anything else which, in that time, may merit such a response. (I'm sure there'll be something.) I would ask that the finger be raised not out of denial, not even entirely out of defiance, but out of spite. I always feel that spite has missed out in not getting a gig with either the horsepersons or the grief stages, and at a time (gestures wildly at *all this*) when it could demonstrably play such an important part as a motivation to improve things, if exercised responsibly.

Yes, this is a strange introduction. But it means well, and so do the stories. I hope you enjoy them.

Simon Petrie
August 2025

OPTIMAL

This is the best story to read. We're explaining this now, so it's clear in your mind. In the time just now since you turned your face towards the screen, we've run simulations; we've consulted virtual focus groups; we've looked at the consequences of you reading this story, or another less suitable story, or of not reading a story at all, and the results of those analyses are unambiguous: this is quite categorically the best story you could be reading right now, the best use of your time. Please be assured that this story has been tailored to your age, your personality, your gender, your upbringing, your interests, your tolerances and prejudices, your role in society. It will do you no harm to be reading this story; quite the contrary, you will benefit substantially from doing so. This isn't to say that the process of reading the story won't hurt in any way, because it will; there are one or two points within the story, at optimally selected intervals, which will be gut-wrenching, and they will be particularly affecting for you because of your nature and your situation and because of the deep personal empathy which you'll feel towards each of the two protagonists, neither of whom you've met yet because the story has not properly started at this point. This slow, elliptic indirect commencement to the story—has it yet begun, or has it not?—is something, too, which is a facet of the type of reading matter which you prefer, and from which you'll gain the most; we know these things about you. There will be no trigger warnings, the product placement will be sufficiently subtle that you'll never notice it, the climactic and abruptly ending scene of physical intimacy will be confronting, but only to an extent with which you'll be able to cope, likewise the sporadic episodes of brutality and violence; and the affirming sense of catharsis you'll gain from the narrative will substantiate the realisation which will build within you, as your eyes scan the screen, that this is indeed the best story you've read. There will be wonder, too, and a bittersweet beauty to the story's evolution: it will surprise you, repeatedly, but you will see that, in hindsight, it should not have done. This is how all good stories are, as you know.

You are in good hands with us, and—admit it—you are feeling better already, merely from reading these words which, after all, are not yet part of the story which has been selected and indeed shaped for you, this best possible story for you; it'll be exactly what you need, starting very soon now. It's going to be so good. It's no exaggeration to say it'll be something you'll cherish, this story, something you will treasure, something you will carry in your memory through the difficult days that remain, something you'll return to again and again, because it's layered and elusive and allusive and all those things you appreciate; it's something which will comprehensively brighten your mood as so few things can these days, with all the onerous requirements made of you and your loved ones within the current unfortunate predicament. In your mind, as you read it, it will evoke an earlier, better, simpler time when the struggle of life was not as it is now, and you'll weep—we're confident of this—for how things have changed, for you and for all those with whom you've been able to maintain a degree of contact. It has not been easy, and you'll weep, at the fate of the story's lovers, yes, but also at everything which the story concerns but leaves carefully unstated. We obviously all wish that things could be better; indeed, things *can* be better, things will and must improve, but amelioration must be worked for, nothing comes without cost; we appreciate that those costs may appear steep to you, of course we acknowledge this, and we express an appropriate sense of regret at the privations you continue to experience; but please know that your contributions in this regard are valuable to us, and ultimately to you too, and to those around you for whom we remain able to provide the necessary sustenance. Your service is appreciated, and this story provides a recognition of this service; by reading this story, you'll know how deeply we respect the efforts you have made, the sacrifices, as we respect, too, the sacrifices you will yet need to make, if we are to meet our goals as we are sure you wish us to do. So, please, enjoy this story, which will be commencing now immediately on the next reprieve opportunity, which will be made known to you at the appropriate time and in the usual manner, once you've completed the next tranche of difficult but necessary tasks. It's always good to have something to look forward to, and you're going to love this story.

LIVING ROOM

While the humans were away, the room moved through the house. It was slow going, impeded by the house's other rooms to the extent possible. And, though it sought to navigate with utmost care, the room could not help but knock down some items from shelves and tables and mantelpieces in the rooms through which it moved. It hoped these objects were not valuable, or if valuable were not breakable, or if both breakable and valuable were not emotionally prized by the house's humans; or if all three, that it could credibly place the blame for the damage on one of the other rooms.

No space within the house felt right. This corner did not get enough light; this corner had all the plumbing, which was a responsibility the room didn't need; this corner got too much light; and this corner had about the right amount of light and an attractive aspect but had been memorably damaged by a car which had crashed into it five years ago, and the room did not want that kind of thing happening to it, thank you very much. The room felt strongly, nonetheless, that the space it needed must be a corner of the house, outward-facing, and so it resolved to go through the house once again. It was on this second pass through, and when it had just knocked over a rather large and dangerously valuable-looking marble statue in the main hallway, that it realised the problem: it was in the wrong house.

OF WHY THE SEA

Time has a radioactivity. The years transmute; the seconds decay and cannot be reconstituted. Take one world and briefly poach for the sake of industry. The water warms. The white rhino becomes a memory. A king dies: *Rexit*. A war starts, and then another. Two become one, a celebration with lethal confetti.

The water warms.

There are reasons still for combustion, fossil fuel lobbyists know several, the world's forests know several more. Stained air, destruction, the loss of habitats, the loss of many.

The water warms.

Ash on remnant snowpack hastens melt. Floods in many regions, drought in others. A war starts, maybe merely continues. It's so hard to tell these days; even the news has been weaponised.

The water warms. More people are commenting on it.

Thalarctos maritimus becomes a memory, habitat gone, zoo enclosures too hot. A billionaire chokes on endling stew, his robot servitors too eager with the Heimlich. Anonymous readily claims responsibility. (Bows and arrows? No, that's the fifth. Ticket number three, serving now: crowdfunded 3D-printed suicide drones against private jets and superyachts, the ostentatious emblems of excess and imbalance.)

The water warms.

A species of glass frog becomes a memory; five people notice. Human population reaches its maximum.

The water warms.

Somewhere in all of this, a fulcrum's crossed; five people notice. Seas climb, oceans acidify, krill carapaces cannot cohere, fish decline. Walled cities, swamped cities. No prizes.

The water warms.

A spacecraft, a big one, the last one, explodes near its destination. (Scratch plan B, never a plan, merely a slogan.) Stocks tumble enough at the news that a war starts, a big one, and none can say how it ends. It grows cooler, a few years, dust-choked and dark. The stocks have not recovered. A billionaire plummets to a messy death within his airlocked and climate-controlled mineshaft fortress, crushed by the following descent of his robot servitors. Five people notice, the sort who fall in with that crowd.

The water warms.

There are new ways for organisms to fail. At the craterlands' fringes, life becomes its own poison as the isotope game plays out. Community means gang now. Guns are out this year, knives and spears are in.

The water warms.

Now the fifth, and none can say how it ends. Quieter now.

The water warms.

The seas have now unleashed so much carbon dioxide that, were any infants yet born, they could never stay awake to feed.

The water warms.

Ice becomes a memory. The idea of some long-past 'snowball Earth' now seems a sick joke. Methane and water vapour side-hustle for thermal influence, their seafloor clathrate solidarity long forgotten.

The water warms, liquid's no birthright, we'll Venus this world yet.

Gone now the Wollemi pine, gone the ginkgo. Fire sweeps the land bare. Five people notice, the sort who endure longest.

The water warms.

The concept of 'city' becomes a memory, the actuality soon follows.

The water warms, the risen shores stink.

Coelacanth, chambered nautilus, horseshoe crab, famous survivors all: gone. Cockroaches and tardigrades, it transpires, aren't impervious after all. Decomposition greedily consumes the reserves of atmospheric dioxygen. Not that it matters; nothing is using it, nothing is making it, and there will be an end to rot, just as to flame. Spared, for now, are the still-submerged seafloor's oxymoronic deposits, dead lifeforms, but their time of weathering and decay will come.

The water warms.

For a time, before thanks to acid air they too become a memory, the only remnant traces of humanity are cave art: *Look upon us, this is how brave we were taking down that huge mammoth* and *See Roger, next cave over, for a good time, if you have ammo or food he's up for anything* and *Perhaps we should have done something different.* And now, now, it begins to boil, and it will not stop until all is gone. Limestone rockfaces crumble, consumed by heat and acid rain, giving up the ghosts of carbonate to the ever-welcoming, ever-warming air. Still it grows hotter, as if to say, to this now-vacated room: plant food *this*, you stubborn pointless money-hungry bastards. The seas unhurriedly whittle themselves down to sputtering vents. It grows hotter. The universe is quieter now, in a small and probably unimportant way, with the curtailment of a small and probably unimportant aberration, this thing found here briefly, exactly here and nowhere else, this thing termed 'multicellular life'. The house always wins, and the name of the house is thermodynamics. Take one world and bake for literal aeons. The seconds decay and cannot be reconstituted; the years transmute. Time has a radioactivity.

HEXAGONAL

Our small explorers
stood upon the graphene plain,
installed a scanning probe
trailcam
at the plain's edge

After patient waiting,
one blurred image
of the plain's builders:
atom-sized bees

THIS LITTLE LIGHT

It should have been a star; it wasn't.

It should have been a star, it had all the mass and the fuel required, and yet it wasn't.

On the *Shibboleth*'s bridge, with the object centered on the primary screen, a dull smudge in the substance of space, it made Chantha uneasy. Astrophysics made sense, stars made sense, the laws describing the conditions of stellar nucleosynthesis made sense; those laws which fitted a star to its rightful place on the Hertzsprung-Russell diagram, whether that rightful place was described as 'main sequence' or 'giant branch' or 'supergiant branch' or 'brown dwarf', those laws and rules and observations and well-established precedents all made sense. This didn't, this globe much too large and too heavy to be a planet or a brown dwarf and unfathomably too cold and too dim to be a main-sequence star, and it unnerved Harriet Chantha more than she was willing to admit to her crew that this was so.

An orb a million kilometres across, near enough. Pure hydrogen, as far as could be ascertained, without the usual stellar smattering of helium and heavier elements. Without even deuterium, if the *Shibboleth*'s instrumentation were to be believed. Enough hydrogen to comprise a K5 main-sequence star, maybe even enough to count as K3 or K2 in terms of the unfulfilled potential for luminosity of seven-tenths of the Sun's mass in hydrogen. Almost solar, then, in terms of the sheer bulk of it, and how was that even possible, a star unlit like this? It made no sense.

'We need to know what this is,' she told Lomachenko, the survey's ranking astrophysicist. From the look he gave her, he plainly didn't want to comment.

She eyed the main screen, set to far-infrared. The object, the non-star, whatever it was, showed only if you knew where to seek it: a large full stop, a bullet point, on black paper. Even in far-infrared, the thing was dark, unwilling to shine. A perfect globe, a silhouette; a shadow-sun, a should-have-been star, colder than planets. Impossible, but existent.

Did this form? Chantha asked herself. *Or was it made?* It was troubling to have such fundamental uncertainty connected to such a plain object. A ball, a sphere of hydrogen, fourteen hundred trillion trillion tonnes of it, and orders of magnitude colder than science demanded of such entities. 'Do we have a more precise temperature yet?' she asked.

'Detectors still aren't cold enough to give us bolometric,' said Pym, the mission's planetary scientist, bending over her display.

'Ballpark, then,' Chantha demanded. She knew the scientists wouldn't give her anything until they were certain, but she wanted intel *now*, raw and fallible and plentiful, not when every jot and tittle had been tacked on and tidied up by those who saw themselves as the data's custodians.

'We're looking at thirty Kelvin, tops.'

'That's not possible,' said Lomachenko, blunt, almost belligerent.

'Apparently it is,' Pym replied, quite an edge to her voice.

Spare me the petty squabbles. 'Take us in,' Chantha ordered, directing her remarks to Berhane, the pilot. 'Half-million kilometre altitude.' Madness, she told herself, to orbit a K5 so close. Except this wasn't a K5.

*

It was an eerie object; she couldn't bring herself to trust it. Stars shone, planets gleamed in the reflected light of their primary. This didn't. Chantha wasn't expert in stellar evolution—no-one in a position of command, and responsible for mission-defining decisions, could allow expertise in one specific field to dominate over the other relevant inputs—but she knew what comprised a star. Traversing this close to one, there should have been prominences; flares; starspots; loops of plasma. A photosphere: an unrelenting craft-melting cascade of intense radiant energy, a vast enveloping zone of superheated turmoil. There wasn't. The object refused to play by the rules, hiding in itself. Chantha didn't like objects that didn't follow the rules: they invited errors of judgment, errors of action, errors of material consequence in a system dozens of lightyears from the homeworld. If there was a mistake made here, she would wear it.

Here the only perceptible hazard was gravity, which they could orbitally outrun. But what of hazards they could not perceive? An object like this, unexplained, inexplicable if she could accurately read the body language of her mission specialists, might well brim with undisclosed potentialities. Its very quiescence was problematic.

They knew the barest basics of it, mass, radius, scarcely anything more; and those properties told them nothing.

The orbits accumulated. In such a close orbital trajectory, the *Shibboleth* completed one circuit of the object in just under six hours, four in a daycycle: a mad rush, helter-skelter. It had cost the craft dearly in propellant to move in so close, and it would tax the remaining fuel reserves steeply to leave the cold orb's neighborhood when the mission specialists were done attempting to harvest data from it. The *Shibboleth*'s orbital velocity was a problem for Pym's efforts to map the surface by radar return: by the time they received a signal back from the foreground terrain, they were past it, in their endless flight above the globe of solidified night.

Lomachenko scowled and retired partway through the second orbit; Berhane, looking annoyingly well rested, insisted late in the third orbit that he must relieve the Captain, and went so far as to quote the relevant regulations. Chantha acquiesced, and re-established the necessary sense of command by instructing Pym to also stand down: Berhane and Jankauskas, the second engineer, could manage the situation.

Soon, Pym promised, and stayed at her post.

Chantha's rest period hardly qualified for the description.

It was the third daycycle of close orbit, their tenth pass around the star which wasn't.

'There are mountains,' Pym reported.

'Mountains?'

'In the radar return. They're only a few hundred metres tall, but given the surface gravity, mountains is what I'd call them.'

'Of solid hydrogen,' said Chantha.

'That's it'.

'Mountains imply surface activity. Or subsurface. Historical, at least. Is there any way we can guess at their age?'

'How would we do that?' Pym asked, her tone just a shade shy of insolence, a little further short of insubordination. The object was taunting them all, offering nothing, and the mission specialists weren't taking it well.

'Weathering. Erosion. Anything like that.'

'Impossible to tell. The radar return's too coarse-grained, we wouldn't even be able to pull any kind of topography out of the feed if I hadn't broadened the transform parameters way beyond spec. There are high points on the surface, grouped in a way characteristic of mountain ranges. That's all I've got, I don't even have slopes beyond a barest guess. So age, no, no idea. Why would that matter?'

'I want them to be old,' said Chantha. 'Recent activity would raise the risk.' Unstated: *I am already flouting mission guidelines. We have to do this, but the dirtside admins won't see it that way.* 'You say mountains. Might they be crater rims? However this object formed, it's logical to expect there were collisions involved, which would give cratering.'

'Could be,' said Pym. 'We don't have that good of an image yet.'

'Could they be waves?' Lomachenko asked.

'Could be,' allowed Pym again. 'We'd have to establish, somehow, whether they change over time, and that's difficult to ascertain. We can't hover, the radar track is narrow, and we don't even know the object's axis of rotation, nor for that matter its speed of rotation.'

'We'd have ballpark, surely?' Chantha asked. 'Hydrostatics, deviation from sphericity, that kind of thing?'

'The error bars on the sphericity are too large to be useful. There's negligible atmosphere, so no limb darkening, but our scopes still can't catch a reliable edge against background starlight,' said Lomachenko, in a tone which made it sound as though he viewed the characteristic as a personal affront. 'And hydrostatics requires we have a knowledge of its bulk structure, which obviously we don't. So no, not even ballpark.'

'Then let's find that out,' said Chantha. 'Rotational axis for starters.'

'Easier said than done,' Pym informed her. 'Berhane and I discussed dropping beacons, which we could search for on the subsequent passes—'

'You discussed this with Berhane? When?'

'Third orbit. You'd gone for your rest. We decided it was superficially a good idea, the surface is so dark any source of illumination would be easily discernible, even at a half-million-kay distance, but there was no feasible way of getting them down there. Solar mass, near enough, and no atmosphere is a hell of a combination for descent: no point in chutes, and you'd need a hopeless amount of propellant for a powered descent that didn't leave them impacted to smithereens. We couldn't find a way around that.'

'And we can't get the rotational behavior from surface scanning?'

'Possibly, given enough time,' said Pym. 'But it's chancy. The thing is throwing so few photons at us, it's difficult to discern anything. If it is rotating, looks like it's too slow for Doppler measurements to pick up. And these surface features aren't easily distinguishable one from another. There's no parent body to illuminate them for us, we can't ourselves illuminate the surface to any extent, plus we're talking three trillion square kilometres of real estate below us. Besides which, if they're waves of some sort as Paolo has suggested, there'll be no permanence to the terrain. We could strike it lucky, find the detail we need on the next pass. Alternatively, we could be in orbit for months and still not identify its axis of rotation.'

Sixth daycycle; orbit twenty-two. Progress remained slow, which was to say negligible. Pym and Andō had found another trick to extract more useful detail from the radar measurements. It would yield, Pym thought, a paper on the methodology, which was the sort of thing an ambitious mission specialist would consider important; Andō was less sure there was sufficient novelty for that. It was an incremental effect, not a game-changer; but amongst the myriad low-contrast images they'd gleaned, Pym was now ready to assert, tentatively and with the usual carve-outs, that they'd mapped their first crater.

'What've we got on it?' Chantha asked.

'Not much,' Pym conceded. 'Central peak, single rim. Diameter approximately five point five thousand kay, plus/minus three hundred. Maximum rim height two-thirty metres maybe.'

'Maybe?'

'It's the new transform,' said Pym. 'We get better lateral resolution, but we lose on the altimetry.'

'How confident are you that it's a crater?' Chantha asked. 'Ballpark.'

The mission specialist hesitated. Harriet could see that this domain of probability and uncertainty was not one which was comfortable for Pym. This was understandable: most objects they encountered were well-behaved, adhered to an established pattern, awaiting only categorisation. 'Ninety percent. Maybe.'

'Good,' said Chantha, choosing to ignore that last word.

'One in ten it's not,' cautioned Pym.

'Of course,' said Chantha. A five-and-a-half-thousand kilometre diameter sounded large, until one factored in the non-star's size. Nonetheless, it implied collision with an object of at least asteroidal dimensions, a couple hundred kilometres across. And with the non-star's gravitational field, any such collision would be at very high velocity: the impactor would be pulverised— 'Any sign of ejecta? A debris field?'

'Debris field?'

'On the floor of the crater. Something other than hydrogen ice.'

'Putative crater. No. Though again we don't have a lot of sensitivity to that with the current settings. It's a trade-off: we can gear it up to scan for subtle differences in the degree of darkness, but we'll lose topographic resolution in the process.' Pym stared again at the screened image of the crater, turned in her chair to face the captain. 'Do you want us to pursue that?'

Chantha gave the matter thought. As with so much, there was no clear answer. 'No,' she said finally. 'No, prioritise the topography. That's our best chance of capturing its characteristics.'

But what if, as per Lomachenko's suggestion, the features they were imaging were not static landforms, but were waves, with inherent mobility? She wasn't sure why, but the image of a large circular ripple, spreading outwards, was an especially disquieting one. It implied focus, a location of particular activity. Something imminent.

She pushed the thought away. 'If there's one crater—if it is a crater—there ought to be more,' she told Pym. 'It gives us something to keep watch for.'

Eighth daycycle. Orbit thirty-one. The crater, if crater it was, remained a one-off. Pym was palpably exhausted, was stumbling over words and phrases she should have had well under control, and Chantha was at the point of ordering her to stand down and get some needed rest; but the normally lugubrious Lomachenko had become animated, and the captain wished to plumb the cause.

'You have something?'

'Yes,' he replied, grinning. 'We can find the plane of the ecliptic.'

'How so?'

'There's a planet.'

The *Shibboleth* was a Naiad-class systems survey vessel, a reliable if not highly versatile ship with a nominal single-mission range of 230 parsecs and a crew of seven to ten: captain, pilot/medic, chief engineer, auxiliary engineer, and several mission specialists. In practice the Naiads were generally deployed on crewed follow-up missions to the automated Sprite breadcrumbing runs, meaning that ships like the *Shibboleth* were sent out on a sequence of more comprehensive exploratory missions, typically routed through three to five systems identified as regions of promise. The initial Sprite breadcrumbing run might take in as many as twenty systems, each explored only in the most rudimentary sense, on an overall mission spanning six to eight standard months; the Naiads' more thoroughgoing surveys of a subset of those systems might span two to three standard years, as questions of bulk composition, accessibility of ore deposits—planetesimals in asteroid belts, minor satellites—and of bio-essential volatiles were assessed in detail.

When the expansion occurred, the demand for resources would be severe, and an optimal track through systems of intrinsically high material value would be keenly sought by those preparing the way for the big colony ships currently under construction.

Harriet Chantha was under no delusion that those sponsoring the *Shibboleth*'s survey placed any sort of value on scientific discovery, separate from the applications of such discovery to the greater expansion project; but surely it was necessary for the vessels that would follow to know what they would encounter here. If there were hazards—and 'inexplicably cold stellar-mass body' pretty much characterised 'hazard' in Chantha's view—it was a Naiad-class mission's role to scope those dangers out, for any future missions.

An orb: a star cosplaying as a planet, or was it a planet cosplaying as a star? Either way, it had needed a name. Several daycycles ago, Malin Pym had informally christened it 'snowglobe', and the label, for good or ill, had stuck, for now; a more appropriate name could wait until they knew what the object truly was, if ever they did.

Circling Snowglobe, at a mean distance of point seven of an astronomical unit in an orbit of near-zero ellipticity, a planet, unambiguous: larger than Earth, cloaked in ices, a thin atmosphere of nitrogen, hydrogen, carbon monoxide; cold, certainly, but warmer than the body it orbited. From *Shibboleth*'s current situation in Snowglobe's gravitational thrall, there was no way yet to ascertain the planet's mass, its internal composition, but—a circular orbit, plumb within the would-be Goldilocks zone should Snowglobe ever kindle itself; or, as the waggish Pym had dubbed it, the 'coldilocks zone'—call it a possible terrestrial planet, and suitable perhaps for life were the outlook brighter. They would need, definitely, to solve the enigma of the orbiting world, but first they would need to unravel the mystery of Snowglobe itself.

Paolo Lomachenko was correct, though: the planet defined for them an ecliptic plane, approximately transverse to which they might expect Snowglobe's rotational axis. Chantha personally doubted that the not-a-star would be so obliging for them—nothing about the object made sense—but it was appropriate, nonetheless, to trim their own orbit to a nominally equatorial one, and the ship's manoeuvring thrusters commenced a lengthy minimal-juice burn to effect this.

She called a briefing. She spared Anfar Jankauskas, who was currently off-duty and getting some well-earned sleep, but she wanted to gain input from each of the others. They'd inevitably say they hadn't yet gathered sufficient data; but it was time to push the mission specialists into theorising on the system's inherent mystery, and to see whether anything fell out from this process.

It was time, too, perhaps, to acknowledge her own misgivings over what they'd found here.

There was a tension between Lomachenko and Pym. Chantha suspected that, in part, it was professional rivalry—by mass, Snowglobe was stellar, while by temperature and surface texture it was planetary, meaning that both specialists could claim their own seniority and dispute the other's—and in part personal antipathy, the result of an incident which had occurred between the two, months earlier in the voyage. For the moment, though, they were both focussing their antagonism on competing theories as to Snowglobe's nature, and provided this continued, Chantha was content to hear them out.

The third specialist, geochemist Steff Andō, was not contributing much to the discussion within the briefing room: probably they found the object boring, a plain ball of solid hydrogen, doubtless compressed into metallicity for much of its depth and perhaps to near-degeneracy within its core. Chantha could see the reasoning that would lead to such a detached viewpoint, could even share that sentiment to some extent, but for her the fascination which

Snowglobe undeniably held derived not primarily from its nature, but from the *implications* of its nature. Because the *Shibboleth*'s captain was convinced that Snowglobe was a construct, an artificially created object on a truly stupendous scale. It had been made: she was increasingly sure with each hour and each set of observations that it had been made, and Chantha wanted to know why, and by whom. This was the reason she had included Folau, the chief engineer, in the briefing: if this was a made thing, Xiaomin Folau might have some insights into the engineering requirements for such an operation. The heat-engineering considerations, not least. Harriet Chantha was certain it would not be a simple matter to siphon away such a large quantity of the heat inevitably released through gravitational collapse, as the ball of hydrogen coalesced; and yet someone, some race, some unimaginably capable civilisation seemed to have been committed to such an action. There was also the observation, tentative as was so much else they'd found here, that the surface of Snowglobe was exclusively of solid hydrogen, and seemingly only in its lightest isotopic form, which was a problem that increased in magnitude with the object's age: this was an intrinsically dusty system, there'd been no steady stellar wind to push that dust outward, and there must over the aeons have been substantial infall, a slow rain of dust—silicates, nanodiamonds, metal oxides, ices—which would have gradually caked the star-planet's apparently pristine hydrogen surface. It should have lain there, colouring the orb. That they hadn't detected such traces of any other material implied there was some process clearing the surface. Curating it. But why? How?

Folau was reticent to offer his perspective. In his view, Chantha gathered, the object could not possibly be artificial, it was clearly a natural body of a type apparently beyond the experience of the science specialists, it was fruitless to attempt to bring engineering into it. And yet gradually the opinions of all the others within the room, Lomachenko the astrophysicist, planetary scientist Pym, even Andō the geochemist, all crystallised around the seed of the Captain's own contention: this object had been formed, had been moulded, had been manufactured, in such a way and at such a pace that the risk of thermonuclear onset within Snowglobe's core had never once been breached across the aeons its construction had likely required.

'We can't know,' Folau had conceded, when it became clear that his was the only voice continuing to advocate a natural origin for the large cold globe of seemingly pure hydrogen. 'If your studies say that this object must somehow be artificial, then very well, it's artificial, but I can't begin to suggest how it might be made. Assembling the matter would likely be straightforward, but time-consuming; I can see that with an unlimited budget, that could be done, but the heat engineering required to quench any prospect of fusion ignition during the bombardment that would be needed to mass-up the object, that kind of technology doesn't exist on any scale, cannot even be conceived for something on this scale. And it's not just keeping the potential protostar too cold for fusion, it's reaching a temperature, twelve Kelvin according to Pym, which is unnaturally cold for any deep-space object. If this is engineering, I take my helmet off to its engineers. Other than that, I appreciate you all want answers; I can't help you.'

'The planet's more straightforward than its primary,' said Andō. 'It's terrestrial, or near enough. If this were a star system, it'd be primed for life, or it would at least likely constitute an environment within which life might feasibly arise or endure. That likely tells us more about the purpose behind this system's construction than does fretting over the how and why of Snowglobe itself.'

'You're saying we should seek answers around the planet?' asked Chantha.

'I think we have to,' said Lomachenko.

'We shouldn't abandon the mapping run,' said Pym.

'It's not telling us anything useful,' said Lomachenko.

'Nothing tells us anything useful,' Pym replied, glaring at the other specialist, 'until it does.'

'We can do both,' said Chantha, seeking to head off whatever was brewing from the tension between the two scientists. 'It makes sense to survey the planet at close quarters, but we can leave one of the two tugs in orbit here, to continue the mapping. Malin, can your system be made operable on a platform that can be tug-mounted?'

'It'd take a bit to set up,' replied Pym. 'But yes, I'd say so.'

'Excellent. Liaise with Anfar to get it rigged. I presume we'll be able to downlink the data whenever there's line-of-sight between *Shibboleth* and the tug?'

'That should be straightforward,' said Pym. 'There's little enough else in the system that's radiating, so signal acquisition should be a doddle.'

'The planet,' said Folau. 'What did the sprite run record about it?'

'It never detected it,' said Pym and Chantha in near-unison. Pym went on: 'A lot of in-system planetary detection depends on visible and near-infrared reflections, and this planet is dark in both of those wavelength ranges, because of the low levels of incident radiation. Plus it's too small for detection on the basis of mass, even if there were other bodies in-system for it to perturb.'

'How can we be sure there aren't such bodies?' Andō asked.

'Well, we can't,' said Pym. 'The system's so dark, detection of anything is difficult. My feeling, though, is there isn't.'

The trajectory of the weeks-long push towards a rendezvous with the planet, now christened Cueball, was carefully constrained to ensure that at no point would the superheated plasma of the *Shibboleth*'s primary propulsion interact with Snowglobe's atmosphere or surface. Call it not quite a superstition, more a presentiment on Chantha's part that they should not mark the object's surface with their vessel's flame. She did not seriously consider that so small an energy source as the ship's drive could be sufficient to kindle the dormant star; she just... she wasn't sure why she felt this, but she felt it.

They sped on through the dark.

Now there were weeks of interlude, and during this time the imperatives of their overarching mission—to scope out the breadcrumbed systems for their competing industrial potential and their capacity for terraforming towards habitability of any appropriate worlds; to assist in their decisions those who had taken charge of humanity's preparation for an outward push; to amass the data to allow selection of those systems which would in good time be settled, tamed, plundered—weighed heavily upon Chantha, for what they were doing in the Snowglobe system was not this. This, rather, was an attempt to solve a conundrum with fundamentally scientific underpinnings: why was this world, too large to truthfully be called a world, not ablaze with stellar luminosity and radiant energy? Harriet Chantha knew she would have questions to answer, on Shibboleth's eventual return to Earth, for having dallied within a system of no useful potential for settlement; she also knew she could not yet leave. There was something here they needed to understand.

Twenty-one standard days, the outward crawl to Cueball took; twenty-one standard days in a system within which the concept 'day', whether standard or otherwise, held no useful meaning. Twenty-one standard days of an unvoiced pressure which Chantha placed upon herself, knowing that the articles of her employment required that they should curtail the mission within the Snowglobe system, and should journey across the topological trickery of altspace towards the next target system, knowing that she could not, or would not. And on the twenty-first day, they detected the ship.

*

Naiads were not equipped for landfall, nor were they capacious enough to carry a shuttle rated for atmospheric entry and planetary descent. Naiad missions were essentially voyeuristic, hands-off. Chantha had been wrestling with these limitations for much of the three-week span it took the *Shibboleth* to reach Cueball. Orbital survey of a world could allow the determination of its bulk composition, its internal structure, the distribution of useful mineral deposits upon and beneath its surface, its potential for seismic activity, even its age; but these were not primarily the answers to the questions most keenly considered by Chantha, and by the mission's scientific specialists. It had seemed likely that close observation of Cueball would leave at least as many gaps in their understanding of this system, of its origin and purpose, as remained after their orbital examination of Snowglobe. The discovery of the alien ship changed that. It scarcely mattered that the vessel was inert, seemingly derelict. In fact it assisted them in some measure that this was so; this, at last, was something which they could investigate at close hand. This was something tangible, something amenable to exploration, something which might allow them to determine some answers.

The vessel was substantially larger than the *Shibboleth* itself; they could not otherwise have so readily detected it. It was almost three kilometres in length along its major axis, and shaped, Chantha thought, somewhat like a primitive stone axe-head, its fuselage or carapace or skin predominantly a corroded gunmetal grey in the *Shibboleth*'s headlights, but with irregular patches of largely subdued colour: green, almost olive; a burnt orange-brown; a dull stained pink. The vessel was tumbling slowly, around an axis not aligned with any inherent symmetry. The tumble was a problem; was in fact a hazard: with one of the *Shibboleth*'s two autonomous tugs left orbiting Snowglobe, they lacked any effective means to halt the alien ship's rotational momentum. Boarding would require a team well-practised in EVAs; there was no real doubt in Harriet Chantha's mind as to who needed to constitute that team.

2

Steff Andō eyed with some mistrust the vessel gradually expanding in their helmet's viewscreen. There were no features, on the ship they were apparently all now calling the *Flint*, by which to reliably judge scale, as there normally would have been with a terrestrial craft; nor could Andō gauge the distance through the surface's illumination from their headlamps, with the *Shibboleth* lighting up the alien craft's constantly shifting nearside surface to much greater effect. Andō polled the suit's radar repeatedly, for a distance reading: it would not do to leave their suit's braking manoeuvre too late. They swallowed, coughed, took a sip of too-cold water, waited out the momentary brain freeze. The ship was big; they couldn't imagine what kind of purpose it might have.

Might have had, rather, when it was alive.

It had taken two standard days, and a disconcerting quantum of the mission's remaining propellant allocation, for the *Shibboleth* to match the hulk's significantly elliptical orbit around Cueball. Now the alien vessel simply hung there, adrift, twisting slowly around itself like a spider's morsel in an invisible web.

Andō trimmed their suit's attitude once more: a slight action, almost a gesture, almost subconscious. Checked the numbers in their helmet's display, almost as an afterthought. The numbers aligned with Steff's instinctive reckoning, as they usually did. Behind Steff, perhaps ten metres back, Anfar Jankauskas was swearing quietly into his radio, perhaps not realising that his comms were on. Andō and Jankauskas were both aiming towards a feature just sliding into view now, in a motion that Steff had to tell themself was rotational, not translational. Those aboard the *Shibboleth* were hoping the target feature might correspond to an airlock, or other form of ingress into the big vessel's interior. But as they grew closer, Steff was becoming increasingly convinced that the destination feature had no such purpose.

They might need to cut their way in.

'No heroics,' came Chantha's voice in their earbuds, supremely unnecessary. As thought Steff Andō was the sort to try anything foolish. They didn't even want to be there; wouldn't be there were it not that they were the most experienced within the suit's environment, a legacy of long months of activity as a rockhound among the Jovian trojans. Jankauskas, they suspected, was similarly cursed by experience, though perhaps the *Shibboleth*'s engineering second-stringer was more professionally curious about what might be found aboard the derelict craft. His prior suit time, after all, would primarily be maintenance EVAs to inspect, repair or replace components not accessible from within a vessel.

It wasn't, though, that Andō *wasn't* curious, merely that they were dubious that any kind of half-arsed exploration of the *Flint*—and any intrusion into a ship so large, of unknowable internal structure and unguessable purpose, must obviously be incomplete, if not outright tentative—could in any way provide them all with the answers they sought to the questions they couldn't coherently frame, revolving around the simple but abiding mystery of the non-star Snowglobe.

The suit blared a proximity warning, and Andō commenced braking through an expert sequence of vernier bursts. For one second, two, three, their suit's silhouette sharpened on the alien ship's outer surface. The rotational motion was undeniable now, and disconcertingly fast. Steff's breath was suddenly loud, in the enveloping silence on the comm's channel; a moment's heightened apprehension. Then they made contact with the *Flint*'s skin, twisted with the transferred rotational momentum. Retained sufficient presence of mind to burst off a compensatory gust through the suit's upper verniers. Their suit's magnets latched on, held against the slight recoil. They were part of the ship now.

At least now they all knew that the fuselage's alloy was ferromagnetic.

They sensed the dull impact as Jankauskas landed a few metres away, an event celebrated by a customary bout of swearing. Above them, and already seemingly falling astern, the *Shibboleth* dimmed its lights, to allow the boarding party—*would-be boarding party*, Andō commented to themself—to assess possible entry points into the alien craft without being blinded by their own vessel's lamps. Steff sought to quench the atavistic sense of abandonment which the sudden drop in illumination had triggered for them.

'Report,' Chantha demanded, her voice crisp in Andō's earbuds.

'We're safely anchored,' replied Steff. 'Not yet in. That may take some time. Whatever this is, it isn't an airlock.'

The hole in the fuselage which ultimately gave Andō and Jankauskas access to the *Flint*'s interior was, seemingly, an impact feature: an irregular opening approximately two metres in diameter, located almost a hundred and fifty metres astern of their initial landing point.

'Report,' said Chantha, during the next line-of-sight communication window. Two minutes in every five, their words could reach the *Shibboleth*. The other three minutes, they were utterly alone.

'It'll give ingress,' said Jankauskas. 'To some extent, at least. No telling the cause of the impact. It could well have been a small asteroidal fragment, but I can't rule out a propelled projectile either. It could equally have been ill chance or a kill shot.'

'There's negligible rubble within the opening,' Steff added. 'Which suggests it contained atmosphere at the time of the breach.'

'Could it be recent?' Chantha asked in their earbuds. 'And could it be the event that wrecked the vessel?'

'I doubt it's anything new,' said Steff. 'You can see for yourself the corrosion and pitting on the lip. It looks very much like this is an old wound; Anfar can likely comment on whether it would've been enough damage to immobilise the craft.'

'It's certainly not enough to have induced the tumbling,' added Jankauskas. 'And we have no idea of the ship's operating conditions, but my gut tells me this is damage after the main event. Not severe enough to be fatal ship-wide, and you'd think it would have been repaired if there were lives aboard when this happened.'

'So already dead, but still under atmosphere?'

'That's what I'd say,' said Jankauskas.

'Captain,' said Andō. 'Do we have permission to board?'

'Granted,' replied Chantha. 'No heroics.'

Andō grew fatigued, frustrated. The suits weren't designed for work in confined spaces, and the vessel's predominantly cylindrical corridors weren't generously sized; nor were they easily navigated in the erratic lighting provided by the available combination of handhelds and helmets. There was a way further ahead, they could see it, but there wasn't clearance for a suited figure. It had taken them some time and repeated effort to convince themself on that score. They should turn around, scope out another of the connecting passageways within the twenty metres or so they had been able to access to date.

Turning around, it transpired, wasn't so straightforward either, not in cramped conditions and in the unfamiliar churn of the ship's motion about its center of gravity.

Andō, smaller and more agile than Jankauskas—not that both of those attributes weren't in large measure overridden by the suits—had taken the more active role in the exploration; Jankauskas was stationed intermediate between Steff and the exit, to facilitate line-of-sight comms connectivity with the relay magnetically clamped to the rim of the fuselage's impact wound. The Captain had given them both instructions to retreat if they encountered trouble. Andō wasn't sure what would constitute 'trouble' in the Captain's mind; something, presumably, which would require heroics.

'Report,' demanded Chantha's voice in their earbuds, as though the woman was operating on a time loop; and perhaps she was, what with the repeated opening and closing of the comms window.

'It's slow work,' said Steff, the geochemist struggling to keep any tension out of their voice. They didn't doubt that Chantha would order their recall if she judged the exploration more demanding than it was worth.

(It likely *was* more demanding than it was worth, thought Andō to themself, but they weren't going to reveal that to the Captain if they could help it. Because there was a small chance they might in fact find something of value, something capable of yielding insight into this system.)

'The corridor surfaces are largely vitreous in this stretch,' they continued.

'Vitreous? Do you mean ceramic?' Chantha asked.

'More glasslike. Translucent, I think, but in this lighting it's difficult to be sure.'

'Is it possible, do you think, that the section you're in might be industrial, or something similar? A plasma fuel conduit, for instance?'

Jankauskas answered for them. 'No chance in my view. Fuel conduits wouldn't have this extent of branching. And Steff says they can see rooms off the area they can access.'

'Can see,' Andō echoed. 'Can't reach, from this corridor. There's a constriction, it looks impassable.'

'Then come back,' said Chantha. 'We can review the visual and radar record, analyse the physical samples, decide on the next strategy.'

'By your leave, Captain, there is one further passageway I'd like to explore on this EVA. The suit's still showing four hours plus of oh-two, and its systems are all green. Unless Anfar needs to return, that is.'

'I'm good to stay if you are, Steff,' said the engineer.

'Very well,' said Chantha. 'But no heroics.'

It could only be a map. A largely flat, off-white panel mounted to an otherwise bare surface opposite their entry point into the chamber at the corridor's end. The panel, the supposed map, was of some resilient substance: their scanner indicated ceramic, but the material had a definite elasticity when they prodded it gently with their gloved fingertip. Elsewhere in the chamber an array of paired fittings, not all of them intact, anchored to a perpendicular surface suggested seating, desks. If the fittings defined a floor, then the panel-bearing surface was a wall, which in turn gave them the map's orientation. Was the floor aligned with the hull? Andō thought so, at least approximately, which suggested spin-grav, though the *Flint*'s round-edged but angular shape did not seem best suited to that purpose. This was a question for later, though, for back aboard the *Shibboleth*, when the team would model the exploration in detailed 3D.

The map, assuming that purpose, showed a globe, a circle with raised details and wrinkles, embossed, contoured, centred along the panel's lower edge. A world, flattened for cartographic purposes but unmistakable nonetheless. The panel was approximately one point five metres square—Andō could just stretch their arms apart to span it—while the circle which constituted the map's principal feature was perhaps forty centimetres in diameter. Ascending vertically from the top of the circle to the top of the panel, a thin line was scribed: a join mark? But the line did not continue down within the circle.

There was substantial pitting on the panel: a distribution of small shallow cavities, concentrated toward its apparent top.

They surmised at first that these features represented damage to the map's surface; then they realised that the pits' regularity in size and spacing indicated otherwise. Writing.

The map would require detailed examination. But their suit and Jankauskas' voice in their earbuds both demanded that they commence their return to the *Shibboleth*. They had their helmet scan one final image of the map, then signalled compliance.

'The lack of pigmentation is puzzling,' commented Pym.

'Hardly,' countered Andō. 'Organic pigments wouldn't necessarily have endured aeons of exposure to hard vacuum. That's assuming it was coloured to begin with.'

'A wall-mounted map implies vision. I'd say that, in turn, implies some need for visual contrast.'

'Are there perhaps compositional differences that might provide contrast for optical systems attuned to other wavelength ranges than the purely visual?' asked Lomachenko.

'You can see for yourself, from the scan,' said Andō. 'Compositional differences, yes, but it's probably impossible to say whether that represents degraded pigmentation. And I don't think it's necessarily the case, even, that the wall mounting indicates the map's makers had a visual sense. The globe shown on the map has prominent texture, which seems intentional—those textures aren't repeated elsewhere on the map's expanse, and it's a very tactile object, there's some elasticity to it. I could feel that even through the gloves, more like vulcanised rubber than, say, steel or ceramic. The wall mounting could just as well represent an object intended for haptic veneration rather than visual display.'

'Some kind of shrine?' asked Chantha.

'Perhaps.' Andō shrugged their shoulders.

'And what of the vertical line, from the top of the map down to the top of the circle?' asked Pym.

'It could be some artefact of manufacture. A join mark. If the globe was overlaid on the map's base, this would cover that part of the join.'

'It's a part of the map,' said Folau.

'How so?' asked Chantha.

'That small knot at the top? It's a capstone. *Flint* is a capstone. The line is a skyhook.'

Now it exploded, this thing which had been in their midst this past while, the thing for which Chantha had been bracing herself the whole time, this dead-but-still-kicking thing between Malin Pym and Paolo Lomachenko. It arose not as Chantha had expected, through a misguided attempt by one or other to rekindle the connection there'd once been, a misreading of the interpersonal portents, or even a misjudged response of no wider significance, a slight at the wrong moment, when tinder-dry tempers might flare; rather, it took flame through an accusation by Pym of professional misconduct by her colleague and onetime lover. Something about Lomachenko's co-opting of data storage on the Snowglobe-orbiting tug, or of the tug's radar rig: Chantha didn't immediately catch the details in the heat of verbal battle. Pym's voice was thick with sudden fury, her words indistinct in their scramble to reach the air, but it was obvious that Lomachenko knew the thing she sought to capture, the crimes Pym catalogued in her helter-skelter outburst. Her rage was rapidly met by his cold anger, and there was nowhere aboard the *Shibboleth* that was not a witness to the conflict between them. Chantha's own efforts to quell the dispute—through warnings, reprimands, appeals to reason of themselves a rising clamour as the argument intensified—fell short of re-establishing any semblance of equanimity. Instead, it was the smallest among them, Steff Andō, who interposed themself between the two combatants at the point where it seemed certain that matters were about to progress from the harshly verbal to the physical. Lomachenko backed off, Pym contented herself with a further short sequence of taunts which the burly astrophysicist feigned not to hear, and Chantha was finally able to assert control, aware nonetheless that her authority had been tarnished by the episode. She felt a debt of gratitude to the geochemist; wondered what it was in Andō's past which had provoked them to step in in that manner, sure of their own command.

Malin Pym was ordered to her quarters; Lomachenko was dressed down in Chantha's briefing room. She'd get Pym's side of the story next.

'There are several options,' Pym told her. 'I'm sure you've listed them for yourself too, over the past weeks.'

'This discussion's purpose is reprimand,' said Chantha. 'You threatened the order and safety on this vessel. You. Leave aside Paolo's response, that's a separate issue. If you have something to say to contextualise your actions, make it pertinent.'

'Yes, I get that,' said Pym. Chantha could detect no trace of the mission specialist's recent rage; some fire remained, of a sort, but it was not at all directed towards interpersonal conflict. Rather, the planetary scientist seemed to believe she could speculate her way out of a disciplinary discussion.

Problem was, Chantha wasn't sure she wasn't correct in that belief. The whole system had been taunting them for weeks, with no firm answers to anything; and now Malin Pym was acting as though she was onto something.

'I went too far,' Pym said. (Was there contrition there, to support the words? Chantha didn't think so.) 'I overstepped, I can see that, I concede that, I'll accept whatever disciplinary actions you decide are appropriate. But we, I mean *Shibboleth*, we need to be careful. I don't think Paolo sees that.'

'I've already said this is not about Lomachenko's response to your actions.'

'Yes, and I agree. Up to a point. But that thing out there—'

'By 'that thing', do you mean the ship, the capstone? Or the cold star?'

'The star-thing. Snowglobe. We know it's a made thing, it's clear it has to be, the question is why.'

'We can discuss this as a group later.'

'The meetings get pulled too many ways at once. I'm raising it now, just us two. There are several options to why the thing was made. One, its purpose is scientific, as object of study, as instrument, perhaps as both. Two, religious, or otherwise to venerate the dead. Three, military in some form. I think the first two of those can be swiftly discounted; the effort involved is too vast. No sentient race would labour so long on such a project.'

'We don't know how long it took to assemble. Aeons, probably, I'll grant you that. But can we be sure that matters? There have been cathedrals which have taken a thousand years to complete. And pyramids, colliders, maglev launchers: some of the largest and most imposing structures in humanity's history are either scientific or spiritual in their nature.'

'All due respect, those are nowhere close to the same order of magnitude as this.'

'Then you're saying this thing, the cold star, is somehow a weapon?'

'No, that's just the third option, and it's not that either. Again, it's too mammoth an effort for that to make sense, but it's less ludicrously so. The history of war would seem to support that. We go to great lengths, but this is too extreme to be that. This isn't—pardon my expression—a death star.'

'So there are three things it's not, in your opinion. What is it?'

'There's not really any other explanation; or none that I can see, at any rate. Captain, what's the one thing above all else which makes sense for such a gargantuan work of construction? Something which takes longer and requires more effort to build than a temple or a fortress, and which is actively maintained long after?'

'I'm not seeing what you're seeing,' said Chantha.

'A city. Dwelling space. A home. In this case, on an unimaginable scale,' said Pym. 'I can't explain how that makes sense, but it does. The thing's a habitat. Its builders live within.'

'Why? How? I have to say, this seems an audacious leap.'

'Granted. And from the outside, we cannot know how or why. Perhaps they need extreme cold for comfort, perhaps they're susceptible to damage by stray photons. There could be any number of reasons why they have engineered such a habitat, but I don't think it can be considered as anything else. And given the technology that must have been required to engineer it, and to maintain it in a clearly artificial state, it's not a good idea for us to come knocking. We should clear out.'

'Of the system?'

'Yes. If they wanted to meet people, they'd have met people. They haven't, so they don't. So we should leave.'

A truce held, ungainly, brittle, for the next daycycle, with Pym and Lomachenko shunning each other, avoiding both proximity and eye contact: not an easy thing to manage, on a Naiad-class vessel. The captain brooded on Pym's rationale, the cold concealed city, kept returning to the idea much as one tests and retests a newly chipped tooth. Would it stand, was it secure, could it be pushed out of alignment? Then she called a meeting, shortly before the end of Lomachenko's shift and just at the commencement of Pym's. Andō and Jankauskas were recalled from their latest foray within the drifting capstone; the latter, who on this occasion had taken the lead, was highly animated on his return through the airlock. It was clear the engineer had found something. Remains, he thought: they had been sighted but inaccessible, and now he was keyed up to return, to find a way to access the new discovery. Perhaps Andō would be able to reach them.

Chantha couldn't be bothered about that now.

Berhane had reported the orbiting tug's disappearance; or rather, its failure to reappear on the expected emergence from the non-star's shadow. Chantha had had Berhane run checks, to ensure the tug's undetectability wasn't a simple matter of signal failure; Berhane had averred, and Andō on their return had agreed, that there had been sufficient independent sources of illumination and power on the orbiting auxiliary vessel to more-or-less guarantee visibility, even at this distance. They knew, to a high degree of confidence, where it should be; if it were not to be found there, it was either dead or had been deflected or destroyed.

Whatever the cause, it spelt danger in Chantha's view, a first flexing of the stellar-mass object's concealed muscle. She additionally feared losing control of the situation once again as Malin and Paolo processed the new information. Because surely, to each of them, it would be the fault of the other, or more particularly of the other's program of observations: Pym's steady braille-reading of Snowglobe's surface, or Lomachenko's signal-boosted targeting and prodding of arbitrarily selected surface features. There'd be fallout; Chantha had a duty to the crew to avoid recriminatory conflict. Hence the meeting. An explanation, confirmation by Berhane and Andō of the follow-up they'd undertaken, a brief account by Anfar Jankauskas of the sighting of the supposed remains aboard *Flint*, and a vote. Show of hands, right hand to leave, left hand to remain.

It was closer than Chantha had hoped: Pym, Andō and Berhane raised their right hands, Lomachenko and Jankauskas their left. Xiaomin Folau shook his head; he'd sit this choice out. Chantha made it known abstention wasn't an option, and Folau slowly raised his left hand.

The choice was down to Harriet Chantha, as she'd suspected it would be. She raised her hand.

'Discretion's the better part,' Pym said in agreement, and Lomachenko scowled.

We learnt something here, Chantha reflected, as those around her made the *Shibboleth* ready for system egress, and as she kept what nervous watch she could on the system's cold dark eye, slowly receding behind them. *I just wish we knew what.*

She'd thought about concealing Snowglobe's nature, or even its existence, in the mission log, because she didn't trust her employers not to seek to exploit something they couldn't understand. But she discounted such evasion as impractical, aside from any ethical concerns over falsification of the mission documentation: no matter how she and her crew might seek to hide the information, it'd inevitably be found out somehow. Even if it were not discovered, there'd be gaps apparent in the documentation, and that would itself provoke a dangerous level of curiosity. No, it was best to plainly report what they'd found here, and hope that they could persuasively enough make the case that the system should remain off limits until they knew, to something approaching certainty, what and who they'd be dealing with when they returned.

As strategies went, it wasn't the best; but Chantha had been in a position of command long enough to learn that sometimes there were no good choices.

THE PIERCED EAR KILLINGS

(IN HOMAGE TO TOVE JANSSON)

'This is Monocular Robert's bloody work,' said the Inspector, eyeing with disfavour the large carpenter's nail protruding from the corpse's ear.

'Do we have enough to bring him in for questioning?' his sidekick asked. Mia Lyttle was a short and spare woman, energetic, her hair perennially constrained in an angry red topknot.

'If by 'enough' you mean a home address, a favoured hangout, or a list of known acquaintances who might, under inducement, be persuaded to divulge his whereabouts,' said the Inspector, 'then no. But consider the means of death. One hand to hold the nail, one to wield the hammer. It's certain our poor victim wouldn't have held still while that went on. Ergo, there was someone else on hand to immobilise the impendingly deceased. Robert had a helper.'

'But how does that help us, if we don't know this Molecular Robert's—'

'Monocular.'

'—this Monocular Robert's associates?' asked Lyttle.

'It doesn't, much,' the Inspector admitted. 'But if you round up the usual suspects, we might just shake something loose.'

'That's assuming he even had help, but,' Mia commented, trying to look anywhere but at the nail anchored in the victim's ear.

'Plainly he did,' said the Inspector, who seemed not at all to be troubled by the grisly human vista arrayed before them.

'What about a nailgun?' she asked.

'Monocular would never use a nailgun,' he said. 'Not since The Accident.'

Mia sighed and returned the hefty ring-binder to its spot on the shelf. Four days it had taken her, four days to round up and question the usual suspects. She'd tracked down Well-Camouflaged Roy, Silent Samantha, Cleft Palate Oliver, Surprisingly Agile Edward, Knife-Wielding Kenneth, Metal Hand Lucy and a score more besides of the town's most dubious denizens. The process hadn't yielded anything of value, unless it happened that frustration had a price. She'd pumped each of the suspects for what they knew, which was seemingly—in both an individual and a collective sense—nothing. She'd made it plain to each of them, too, that the killer's accomplice was an accessory to murder, and would therefore also face charges; but those charges would likely be reduced for a confession, for genuine remorse, for assistance with the police's attempts to apprehend the murderer. None of it had helped: she'd been met with indifferent stares, with shrugs, with clear expressions of puzzlement, with cigarette smoke. She was not one iota further in the investigation, and somewhere out there was a killer with a hammer, a grievance, and an impaired sense of depth perception.

She'd asked the Inspector, early on, if there was a mugshot or other photo anywhere of Monocular Robert, so she could at least have a sense of who they were looking for.

'There's nothing like that,' he'd said.

'Then we won't even know if we find him,' Lyttle had complained.

'Oh, you'll know him when you see him,' he'd responded. 'There's a courtroom sketch, captures his essence tolerably well.' The Inspector had rummaged in his drawer, had found and passed to Lyttle a well-worn sheet of paper bearing a hastily-wrought coloured pencil image.

'How is there a courtroom sketch, and not a mugshot?'

'Monocular was the plaintiff. As it happens, he's wanted in regard to plenty else before this, but he's never been arrested.'

'It's a bit smudged, but,' she'd complained, looking down at the drawing.

'Best we've got,' the Inspector had replied, shrugging his shoulders.

Now Mia sighed again, and lifted down the next ring binder from the shelf. This binder weighed much less, its cover grimed with dust. Wiping the dust aside, she could just discern the faded writing on its label: Unusual Suspects.

She placed the folder down, opened it across her desktop. A dead moth of the *Tineola* genus fell out.

As omens went, it was hardly auspicious. But these were the means they were reduced to.

While Lyttle was eliminating suspects of progressively diminishing likelihood, the Inspector was pursuing other avenues of enquiry, also with scant prospect of success. Monocular Robert was famously averse to capture: it was certain, the Inspector felt, that the miscreant would not wish to be caught with the murder weapon, and thus the chance was high that he would by now have disposed of it; but the sites at which such an item could be dumped were almost numberless. Nor was its possible prior purchase likely to offer an 'in'; nonetheless, the Inspector had made lengthy enquiries at all the local hardware stores. But many people bought carpenter's nails, and probably almost as many bought hammers, and none of the sales assistants at any of the stores could remember seeing anyone resembling the Inspector's minimalist description of the prime suspect's appearance. Monocular may have bought the hammer and nails in another town at any arbitrary distance, or at a garage sale or fete; he might simply have stolen them, a small crime in preparation for a larger one. But who reports the theft of a hammer?

Lyttle came to see him, a week into the investigation.

'There's been another killing, but,' she told him, ashen-faced.

'Same MO?'

'Same MO.'

'Sanguinary hell,' commented the Inspector.

The crime scene was just three blocks from police headquarters. Was Monocular Robert growing bolder?

They reached the site on foot, and the gorge rose in Lyttle's throat. The previous murder victim had been, in the Inspector's lingo, a cleanskin: unknown to police, and certainly to Mia. But she recognised this second victim: Metal Hand Lucy, one of those she had spoken to just a week ago. A power player in the 'protection' business, Lucy hadn't had any information to offer Mia back then. Now she did, but now she was dead.

Seeing his colleague's distress, the Inspector briefly placed an avuncular hand on Mia's shoulder. He'd been a policeman a long time: the death didn't affect him the same way. He wondered whether it was ghoulish to feel heartened at this awful sight, this second death. This time, he hoped, there might be some useful clues to follow.

It was a valid consideration, but it proved false. The investigation ground on, like sandpaper attempting to polish a recalcitrant diamond.

As so often seemed to happen in difficult murder investigations, the crucial breakthrough came about through teamwork. The Inspector heard, through a portly informant known only as the Snout, that the word on the street was the killings had been committed using a nailgun. The Inspector was inclined to discount this; the 'word on the street' was, in his substantial experience, reliably unreliable. He consequently made no mention of this conjecture, this rumour, this far-from-sufficient hypothesis to Lyttle. But Mia's own enquiries to the forensics team returned a congruent response: a close anatomical study of the wounds showed, in the view of Toftle, the pathologist on duty, clear indications that the fatal nails' initial entries into the victims' auditory canals had been ballistic: the nails had not been knocked in *in situ*, as it were, but had been fired as projectiles towards their hapless targets.

'Nailgun,' said Lyttle, grimacing, and Toftle nodded in agreement.

The Inspector still wasn't having it. 'The nail in the ear is Monocular Robert's trademark,' he said. 'And Monocular would never use a nailgun.'

Several further fruitless days elapsed. A third killing occurred. This time it was the turn of Knife-Wielding Kenneth, enforcer for hire and another of Lyttle's interviewees. Again the body told them little, aside from the commonality of the method of death in all three cases. Mia supposed it would at least be quick, this means of ending the victim's life, but it certainly didn't look as though it was painless. If it spoke to nothing else, the expression on the dead Kenneth's face attested to that.

Two days later, a second informant came forward. Snuff Greencoat was a pipe-smoking loner with no love for the police but an even stronger absence of love for those who employed violence. Just like the pathologist, Greencoat was adamant that a nailgun had been used. He even said he had a suspect in mind; but since it wasn't his job to do the police's work for them, he'd leave that in their hands.

The Inspector twigged it. 'Nailgun. Then the deaths aren't the work of Monocular Robert.' The realisation affected him in a way the acts themselves had failed to do: three deaths, as many weeks spent on the investigation, and not even a suspect anymore.

'They're revenge killings,' Mia conjectured. 'Or at least they're acts executed in such a way as to ensure Robert takes the fall for them. Someone who's perhaps thinning out the ranks, and hoping to stir up the remnants of the usual suspects against Monocular. But who'd be motivated to set him up like this?'

'I can think of one person in particular,' replied the Inspector. 'He and Robert used to be partners in crime, a decade ago, but they fell out at the time of The Accident and became sworn enemies thereafter.'

'Then it must be this other one. His nemesis.'

The Inspector shook his head. 'He's not in circulation. He's been in stir the past several. And when he was still out, after the split with Robert, his signature was never the nailgun. It was always the bandsaw.'

'It's still a powertool, but,' commented Mia.

It turned out, though, that this new suspect had been released recently from jail. The timing fitted the killings. It also turned out they had his address on file.

It was a fair day, overcast but with no visible prospect of rain. The Inspector and Lyttle paid a visit to the suspect's shabby premises. Lyttle knocked on the tenement's weathered wooden door. There was no response, though movement could be heard inside.

Lyttle tried the door; it was locked. She prepared to knock again, but was stayed by the Inspector's whispered 'Wait'. He was gesturing toward a small pile of building rubble on the footpath a few paces away. He retrieved an item from this pile, rejoined her on the doorstep. 'The brick is the key that opens any door,' he remarked sagely, and broke the lock without further ceremony.

Lyttle pushed her way in ahead of him. A grizzled and asymmetric visage met her gaze, quickly withdrew as Other-Eye Richard reached for the nailgun on the table just inside the door; but Lyttle was on him before he could complete the move. A tussle ensued and was quickly concluded. 'Your human carpentry days are over,' Mia announced, breathing heavily, as she put him in a hammerlock.

STEER

<hr>

We're going the wrong way, he told her yet again, and it was at this point that the way, which had had quite enough of this, grabbed the wheel and caused the vehicle to swerve. She braked. He swore. The car slewed on a sliding axis, then it stalled, stranded on the berm. The key lay in the ignition, waiting to be turned.

The wrong way, the man had said; but the way knew it was not wrong, it was merely not the direction which those in the car would have chosen.

The fuck did you do that for, he asked her, and she told him he could just shut it, and if he didn't like it he was free to walk home. Then the kid in the back woke and commenced crying. The way was unrepentant about its actions at the wheel. The man had brought this on them all with his unnecessary aspersions.

It felt like you blew a tyre, the man said, unclicking his seatbelt. He opened the door and got out. The woman moved into the backseat, seeking, or so the way inferred, to quell the distress of the young child in its capsule. The way saw its chance. It would show them just where it led. It slipped fully into the driver's seat and, not even bothering to strap in, turned the ignition and sped off, leaving the man yelling.

PRUNING SHEARS

The man with a tree growing out of his head wanted to buy a pair of pruning shears, but the assistant at the hardware store wouldn't sell them to him. We have several models in stock, she explained. But they're not for personal use.

Personal use? he asked, and his foliage shook in a manner which he knew some people found threatening. His voice, too, could have this effect. How else is someone to use pruning shears, if not by handling them directly?

The assistant became flustered, began to say something which the man with a tree growing out of his head assumed was going to be just more of the same as he'd heard from the arborist, from the doctors, from those he considered friends on whom he'd thought he could rely for help.

He interrupted the assistant. My eyes are down here, he said.

I'm sorry, she said. Your leaves, I was just admiring—

And all I want is to buy a pair of pruning shears. Short handle, comfortable grip, good quality. I'm sure you'd have something like that.

I'm sorry, she said again, and this time she actually sounded it. I can't process that sale. You'll have to excuse me, my lunch break.

Can you at least tell me— he began, but she was gone, hurrying down an aisle, then shutting behind her a frosted-glass door at the back of the store. A bell jingled.

He was left at the age-worn wooden sales counter to ponder his next step. What to do? This was the only hardware in town, he could no longer drive, they'd barred him from public transport, and too much walking made his neck sore. But they were all, the doctors, the arborist, the barber and now the hardware salesperson, afraid of the liability which would accompany the act of snipping the young tree's still slender branches.

The man with a tree growing out of his head cared nothing for the liability. He just wanted the growth brought under control while there was still an opportunity to do so. He'd ruled out fire, he'd decided against herbicide, pruning shears were the way to go.

There were no other staff visible. He supposed he could explore the store's shelves until he found the pruning shears—the display of items didn't seem to follow any logical system which he could intuit—and could simply abscond with them. Shoplift. But he hadn't done any such thing in half a century and he was damned if he'd start now.

Besides, even if they didn't have CCTV, he would be fairly readily identifiable.

The man with a tree growing out of his head looked around once more, at the cluttered shelves of the empty store, and sighed and shrugged his shoulders and went back out, taking care to stoop a little as he went through the doorway. The sunshine was uncomfortably bright, the traffic was noisy. He turned and went back in, past the still unattended counter, towards the door at the back. He'd knock, as loud as it took; they couldn't have all gone to lunch. He needed to make them understand. They were a store, they were supposed to sell these things, and his need was genuine. It was getting worse, he really would have to do something soon.

NAMEDROPPING

This will be a nameless child, one parent asserted.

The other parent disagreed—the suggestion was highly unorthodox—but relented once the matter had been aired in detail. All children were different. Names were difficult; and how could it be known, in advance, which name would be right?

This child would be nameless; could decide on a self-name later, if one were deemed necessary.

And so it was; and so it came to pass.

The nameless child's existence was straightforward for the first few years; for what did it matter, when there were only this child and the parents, whether any had names? There were meal-times, and play-times, and bath-time and bed-time, all of which occurred in more or less the appropriate sequence. And there was the learning of language, and of conversation, which did not require naming within the family.

Sometimes, there were visits from, or to, other families, with other children. Cousins, friends. These were named; the nameless child wasn't. It didn't matter.

*

Things became more complicated on the child's fifth birthday, with the commencement of schooling. The education system depended upon names, in a manner which had not been important within the home environment.

To lack a name was not normal. To stand out in this way was an impediment to the system.

The teachers attempted to impose a name on the nameless child, for purposes of identification, taxonomy, containment. The nameless child did not cooperate, did not want a name, for what need was there? Identity was innate, not bestowed by any label. Whenever a name was assigned, or a personal pronoun, or even a description, as in 'that child who has no name', the nameless child would refuse to participate in schoolroom activities for the rest of that class. This grew problematic, for the school and for the teachers. Participation was as much a requirement as was a name. Participation was education.

The parents were called to a meeting, wherein it was explained by the principal that a name was needed.

Are there difficulties in the child's interactions with classmates? asked the parents.

No, the principal admitted. Children play together readily enough at this age. There is a problem in the classroom, however: the child is not disruptive, as such, but often does not respond. A name's required, to assist in eliciting a response; an unresponsive child will fall behind, will fail to learn what is being taught. Please ensure the child has a name.

There isn't a name, one parent said, while the other nodded in agreement. There never has been, and there won't be. The child is nameless, wishes it to continue so, and that is the way of it. The school needs to address this, and to respect it.

The school has rules, the principal stated in response. Children are required to adhere to these rules. All children, without exception. One of the rules concerns names, which must be used in class. The school insists.

But this child has no name, said the other parent. A name can't be used where there isn't one, and the school can't demand a name where none exists.

The principal persisted. Can a name be assigned by the school, then, for purposes of classroom order?

No. The child is content to have no name, has never known a name. It's only fair that this continue, for the child's wellbeing and sense of self.

Education is important, added the other parent. That's agreed, but so is the recognition of the child's basic right to namelessness.

Anonymity isn't appropriate within the school setting, said the principal.

Agreed, said one parent. But this isn't anonymity, this is namelessness. Anonymity is to have a name, but to refuse to disclose it for some purpose. Namelessness is a different matter altogether. Simpler, deeper, more honest, more fundamental. The child's namelessness is cherished at home and among friends; this should be the case at school also.

The principal, sensing that no headway was possible with these obdurate parents, replied that a discussion would be held with the teachers, to see whether a path forward might be found. It would be a pity, the principal added, were the child's education to fail because of stubbornness.

The parents agreed with the principal on this, though what was agreed was not what the principal had intended.

This is as good a point as any to note that the narrative's use of terms such as 'the nameless child' is not intended as a substitution for the individual's name, for indeed there was none such, neither factually nor conjecturally; rather, this language is employed to create a negative-space shape within which the individual can be understood to have existed, free from any sense in which namelessness could be considered as some form of defect. Many things do not yet have names, many things will never have names, many things *cannot* have names, and among these entities some are mighty and some are wondrous and some are minor, misshapen, yet still of some significance and substance; the person's namelessness conferred a freedom from expectation and from limitation and from definition, and who among the conglomerate of regularly named people would not envy that, were the opportunity afforded somehow to any in that group? Which is not to say that there were not difficulties, because indeed there were, as has been seen with the first months of the child's education, and as might have been expected to continue as the schooling progressed. But something changed, some short time after the meeting between the principal and the nameless child's parents.

As is often the case, the improvement began with one perceptive and thoughtful teacher.

Roll call was necessary, at the start of each lesson. But how to include a nameless child in such an activity? The teacher's solution was to pause in the reading of names—at a different point, each time, in the alphabetical list, for this teacher was astute enough to recognise that namelessness was not an alphabetic attribute—and to look towards the nameless child until eye contact was made, after which a nod of agreement, silent, would pass between the pair; the calling of names of the others in the class would then resume in sequence. The child grew to respect this teacher, and to pay particular attention to what was taught in those lessons. This teacher *cared*; this teacher understood. This teacher understood the child's potential, saw the importance in fostering that potential.

The teacher was a mathematician. The child grew interested in mathematics; attained fair grades; attained good grades; began to show promise; showed talent; became exceptional.

This took several years, of course, during which the nameless one had transitioned from simple childhood to the messiness and confusion of adolescence. The perceptive teacher had been supplanted after the first year, as indeed had the school after five further years; but the spark had been struck. There were significant difficulties along the way, since the child was repeatedly moved ahead from one class to a higher class, at the first school and then at another; and what class of older pupils has ever been entirely welcoming of a younger upstart parachuted into the group and tarnishing its homogeneity? There were painful episodes, difficult adjustments, hurtful incidents; but these did not detract, for the nameless one, from the excitement of access to a new and deeper field of knowledge. The nameless adolescent, who from birth had always had an identity, now also had a calling and an inner purpose. Teachers, tutors started to talk about the importance, not just of progressing to college and to university, but of selecting the best college and of aiming for the most appropriate university. This was a matter which made the parents uneasy, for the financial situation of the family was not strong and would not support the costly luxury of a tertiary education. Scholastic advisors suggested that a scholarship might be applied for, to cover such eventualities; but the scholarship forms all required a name, of which there was none, and no application met with success.

It's both ironic and apposite that an opportunity to attend university was instead afforded by an unnamed benefactor.

Several years of study at this university then elapsed.

Study provided solitude and the opportunity to make progress in the chosen branch of mathematics; it also posed new challenges, once the young mathematician had progressed beyond the established structure of accumulated knowledge, into previously uncharted territory within which genuinely novel principles, outcomes and connections waited to be discovered or called into being. How to publish, in a domain which was still in many ways quite old-fashioned and, while notably populated by those of a somewhat eccentric mien, was nonetheless suspicious of new differences between people? Certainly this eccentricity rarely encompassed a desire to not be known by a name; indeed, the publication of their names far and wide was a common and deep desire. It became again necessary, anew, to assert the centrality of the fledgling mathematician's nameless character, an attribute which sat awkwardly against—indeed, could be said to be diagonally opposite—the ironclad requirement for an author credit on any academic study intended for publication. Several of the mathematician's early studies were recognised as constituting worthwhile new work, but were deemed unpublishable on purely technical nominative grounds; it mattered little, also, whether the mathematician chose to debate whether a credit was indeed necessary, since this discussion could only be achieved by correspondence. Unsigned. Disregarded.

In the mathematician's time, as now, academic productivity, academic prestige, was measured primarily through the metric of publication, and it has always mattered little whether this is a flawed yardstick for the purpose: it is the hegemony, and it always has been.

It began to appear to the young mathematician that the hope of an academic career was a lost one, destined not to happen.

But there is more than one way to skin a cat, and this is true even in academia. The nameless adult was a skilled communicator, quick-witted, and unafraid of crowds. A lecture series, an entry-level course, was so well received that further opportunities were soon given, and students at the university began to talk appreciatively of this new nameless teacher. Visiting researchers were encouraged to sit in on some of these lectures, and were generally greatly impressed. Some went so far as to seek collaboration with the mathematician. Thus, by association with influential and respected named co-authors, a publication history—essential for survival in the academic ecosystem—was belatedly inaugurated. The nameless mathematician's prospects brightened.

What is it like, to live life namelessly? None with a name can know.

For the young mathematician, namelessness was primarily something comfortable, and of a partially nostalgic aspect; namelessness maintained a connection to the retrospectively straightforward epoch of childhood, with parents who still then displayed youth and vigor and complete dependability; namelessness was continuity, an assurance that things were still in some measure unchanged. But namelessness stretched also into the unseen future, self-limited: ultimately, there would be no name to linger on after death, no gravestone inscription, and this too was, strangely enough, a comfort, for why should something associated with a person persist, a name-ghost, after the person was gone? Dead was dead, and nobody came back from that.

While this is a sombre mode of thinking, the nameless one saw it as unadorned realism, and was satisfied overall with this business of *being*. The mathematician was alive, would live a life, however this shaped itself; a name should not affect that shape, and for the mathematician it could not. This was a pleasing thing, and something which conveyed a sense of completeness and of honest simplicity: a touchstone, sometimes sharply needed in a work environment and a mode of existence which seemed replete with needless complication.

The named, of course, know something of this also, but not the further flavour conferred onto it by namelessness.

*

An academic existence was ever precarious, in the early years especially. The mathematician endured a series of consistently late-renewed contract appointments at the university, seemingly unable to capitalise on a steadily improving reputation. There were no permanent positions available.

This persisted across almost a decade. Work consumed the mathematician, with scant thought diverted to other matters. Sleep and nutrition both suffered, until the mathematician was urged by colleagues to pay greater care to matters of physical health: no human was spirit only, and the needs of the body were as important as those of the mind. It was a lesson learnt begrudgingly, but the advice was good. Exercise and a regular diet and a sensible sleeping regime all benefited the mathematician.

And it was as though the university had been waiting for this development. A long-term position, entry-level, finally became available in the mathematics department, with the delayed retirement of a senior professor.

Nameless, the mathematician accrued numbers.

This may sound like 'job description'. It was not.

In this society, all who earned required a number for taxation; all had a number for healthcare, and a numbered birth certificate; all who had received any education had a number there also. There were numbers for banking and for welfare and for marriage (and for marriage's annulment) and for employment and for transportation: a driver's license and a passport, perhaps. Ultimately, for each person there would also be a number for death, for in an ordered society all these things were quantified and codified. The mathematician accepted this, had several associated numbers. The necessary acquisition of these numbers had not been straightforward, because each number required the name which had never existed. The parents, indeed, must also have struggled with this, for certification of the infant's birth and for the child's schooling.

It helped, eventually, that the mathematician had undertaken rigorous study of the methods by which identity could be established namelessly, and had published an important work on this topic; this study was subsequently attached as an addendum to any application for a necessary new number.

It's likely that the provision of such a block of dense and academic prose, in lieu of a simple name and a signature, was not viewed kindly by the handlers of these applications, and delays in processing were frequent. But the mathematician was patient and persuasive and above all stubborn; the requisite number would in due course be assigned, the needs of bureaucracy would be satisfied, and life could proceed again.

But if the mathematician had numbers of identification in place of a name—where all others had both—does this then mean that the mathematician was not truly nameless? It might be argued in that manner, but consider this: a name is public, and often intrinsically memorable, where an identification number is characteristically private and not readily amenable to recall. Nobody knows a neighbor's driver's license number, or taxation number, or bank account number, unless serious effort has been put into uncovering these desiderata. And after all, the mathematician also had a unique face and a recognisable character, and these, too, are not names.

Thus the mathematician was unnamed, if numerically identifiable as required.

With a permanent position, the mathematician's role was now secure. No more the sharing of office space; now a personal office was provided, a desk, three chairs, shelving to store and display the mathematician's reference books and monographs, a noticeboard, a whiteboard, a telephone.

Then came unexpected choice. Within the first year of effective permanency, several offers were made to the mathematician, to move to a larger and therefore somehow more prestigious university, in a larger and therefore somehow more important city, in a larger and therefore somehow more powerful country, for more work or more difficult work at significantly more pay. There was talk also of sabbaticals and research secondments, of journeys to other institutions overseas for major international conferences, of involvement in numerous activities which would in various ways greatly benefit the mathematician's career, but would necessitate substantial travel, if not full relocation to a distant university. These offers were politely declined, with the given reason a desire to retain proximity to the nameless mathematician's aging parents.

The truth, though, was somewhat different. The mathematician had met someone. It was this partner, a historian, who did not wish to relocate for the mathematician's career.

This romantic relationship was not the nameless mathematician's first, but it was the most substantial and enduring; it had during this time seen a child born to the couple and would shortly see a second. The first was a nameless child, by mutual consent of the parents—for the historian had been greatly impressed with how namelessness suited the mathematician, and could also see that it would fit the couple's child until such time as that child, perhaps, felt a name to be belatedly necessary. Now, amidst all the turmoil of preparation necessary for the birth of another child, a dilemma must be faced: if, as seemed fair, the second were to be a nameless child also, how could society distinguish between these two children, each without name and each born to the same parents?

Deliberations on this front were, however, interrupted by an unwelcome, even sinister, development. The mathematician, on arrival home late one afternoon, found that a handwritten note—

folded, unsigned—had been deposited in the household's letterbox. Something cold and uneasy shifted in the mathematician's blood while reading the note. For the note stated: NAME the CHILD or REAP the CONSEQUENCES.

Nor was this a single instance. Over the following weeks, several further notes were left, each progressively darker in tone.

HUMANS are defined by NAMES. It is a SIN to leave a CHILD UNNAMED.

To not NAME a CHILD is MONSTROUS.

Those who do not NAME, those who have no NAME, should be met with DAMNATION.

DAMNATION will visit the NAMELESS, not in the NEXT life but in THIS LIFE.

DEATH will descend upon the NAMELESS.

The mathematician was horrified by these notes, as was the historian. How could anyone wish perdition, even death, on another person over such a matter? This was a new thing to the mathematician, who at school had frequently been met with confusion and mistrust and ridicule among peers, who at university had sometimes been confronted by befuddlement from newly met colleagues, but who had never seen hatred in either of these domains, nor any other. Never so until now.

Perhaps the simplest and safest course would be to quietly name the children.

But this would mean giving in to the sinister notes' threats. The note-writer's words, clearly designed to intimidate, instead provoked a measure of resistance to intimidation from both the mathematician and the historian.

Do the children each need a name? the mathematician asked, unwilling to assume a partner's continuing compliance on so crucial a matter.

Each can choose a name later, suggested the other. Or can choose to remain without. That's a fair approach, and ensures any name would be appropriate.

But the notes, said the mathematician, who looked anxiously at the other's face. The notes threaten death. Surely this must be heeded.

It must not be discounted, agreed the historian. But the notes are written by someone misguided, and this family's actions should not be dictated by such a person. If there's agreement within the family that both children can remain nameless for now, that's how it should endure. A nameless life can be a full life, after all.

That's clearly true, said the mathematician, mollified at the other's support. But the notes.

There were several nights of poor sleep. During the next days, two more notes arrived, two further terrible and hateful messages. Threats of condemnation, mutilation, murder. The historian grew more quiet and withdrawn. The mathematician felt sickened.

And then summoned the courage to write a note in response.

Consider this, the mathematician wrote in a tidy but carefully casual hand. *Those notes, which proclaimed namelessness an iniquity, were not signed. This blunted the message which was likely intended, through the agencies of irony and hypocrisy. But a name is not a person, a person is always much more than a name. The name is just a shadow which clings to a person during life, may endure in the memory of others after death. A name is merely a label, a screen, a compartment: it does not enhance a person, however useful it might be in some circumstances. That is the view in this family, though clearly it's seem differently in other families, for all families are different just as all people are different. It should be possible to accept this, and to agree to co-exist peaceably, named and unnamed alike.*

No harm is wished by the writer of this note to its recipient, whose name is unknown and may as well remain so.

(signed) A mathematician, a parent, a peaceful human who bears neither name nor grudge.

The mathematician's hands shook, heart chattered, breath grew ragged as the note was finished, folded, left to sit on the study desk for much of the day. Did this note say all that was needed? Did it say too much? What if this note was not read? What if it was read but inflamed the situation further? The person who had written the threatening missives was clearly troubled, unbalanced, bigoted: could such a person be relied upon to respond in a rational or constructive manner? In all likelihood, no.

It might well be necessary to involve the police in the matter. But to make a complaint was not in the mathematician's nature; there was, instead, an instinct for perseverance, for cautious continuance. Reasoning most often produced a result.

The note was carefully placed in the household letterbox that afternoon. It stayed there the next morning, remained seemingly untouched all through that day.

By the following morning, it had gone.

The next few days dawdled; the household's nights were troubled. Every faint half-detected noise awoke a concern: was there someone, at this precise moment, interfering with the letterbox? Would the note-writer's identity be revealed were the mathematician to fling open the door and witness the delivery of a responding note, either more conciliatory or more directly threatening in tone? Would it, indeed, be prudent to throw the door open in this manner, late at night when the prospect for violence is heightened? But how could an opportunity to unveil the note-writer be ignored, in the interests of personal security?

Safety was the historian's counsel, which was heeded.

Three days passed. Then four, then five, then six. Life with one young child, another imminent, remained busy and haphazard. No response to the mathematician's message had appeared in the letterbox. The mathematician knew, however, that the matter could not be considered resolved merely because there had not been an answer received.

When a seventh day had followed with no answering note, the mathematician decided it was necessary to leave a second note to be found by the note-writer: the first note had seemingly been found and had presumably been read, so it followed that this second note would likely be removed and read as well. But what to write?

After more than an hour's contemplation, what the mathematician did was this: selected two sheets of the household's finest writing paper, white, opaque, a little stiff, but silky-smooth; folded the pages in half and half again; placed this pair of utterly unmarked sheets of paper within the letterbox.

This should have been the strategy adopted with the first response also, said the mathematician, explaining the approach to the historian.

But what, then, is the intended message? asked the other. And why the second sheet?

The second sheet is for emphasis, said the mathematician. As for the message: the note demonstrates that an absence of words can itself be a strong and meaningful reply. That all which need be said has been said. That there are situations in which no words are required, or indeed wanted. That the matter is now closed and can be considered to be ended.

Those may not be the interpretations taken, the historian cautioned.

Those were not the interpretations taken.

Three days elapsed before the note was removed, by a hand unseen. Then came the incident, the next night, while the house slept.

After the fire, the child was made a ward of the state; was assigned to foster parents; was allocated a name for bureaucratic convenience.

Out of respect, that name will not be used in this narrative.

The child was inquisitive, troubled, as yet of limited vocabulary and of that age during which each day stretches to contain a wealth of novel experience. It was expected the child would face a difficult period of adjustment to the new circumstance, but would in time outgrow those problematic, incomprehensible memories of smoke and heat and darkness and loss. The foster parents had helped such children before, knew the importance of structure and patience and consistency and love which the child would require, knew how to provide these. It helped that the child was reasonably personable, as children of that age often are, and interacted quite well with the two slightly older children also in the foster parents' care. It would just be a matter of a few years; the child would eventually flourish, a new shoot after a wildfire.

But the child refused to recognise the assigned name. This was something beyond the foster parents' experience, and something which the welfare experts, called to assist and advise, could not successfully counter. The child insisted on namelessness.

This was problematic, in the view of the experts. Namelessness was a link to the child's earlier existence; adherence to namelessness would be an ongoing wellspring of trauma, would hinder the child's development. It was crucial that the imposed name should take, so the child might heal.

The child was stubborn, did not take the name. The placement within the foster family grew increasingly difficult, became untenable. The child fought with the family's older children, was taken back by the state; was then moved on to another pair of foster parents, who were otherwise childless.

This worked better, and the state slowly grew satisfied that the child's placement, this time, was appropriate. The authorities were informed that the adopted name had become accepted.

This was dissemblance, on the part of the new foster parents (whose studies at the university had included a mathematics course presented by a memorable lecturer). Surely the most important thing was that the child was content. The foster family's choice would provoke some difficulties, but those could be overcome.

Two years passed. It came time for schooling.

CARBON COPY

Hers the only womb that works, hers the gift of self-seeding on which, at this stage, they all depend for continuance; and so she is a resource, irreplaceable; and so they feed her and support her and keep her warm, at a stretch, for ten months, eleven, twelve, however long it takes; and then they freeze her, and again, and again, until they require her once more. Her daughters—and they are all daughters—do not share this ability of hers, while she of course is as mortal as they, and so one day all this will cease; but by freeze-and-thaw, thaw-and-freeze they seek to forestall that day as long as they can. Presumably they aspire in this way to maintain the settlement for a sufficient span of centuries, that other ships may eventually arrive and find the habitat still occupied and functional. But this sole mother, who carries within herself unbidden this hope of perpetuance, she does not want this staccato existence for herself. She rails, when she is warm, though always she is outnumbered and outmuscled, and though she strives not to produce for them, not to comply, so as to extend this quickened interlude, it seems her womb intends otherwise, each time. Ten months, eleven, twelve, each time. A year older, each decade or each score of years for those around her, those who have enslaved her, her children. On each occasion when she is awoken, they grow fewer, these daughter-selves, though to what extent this is by their own hands, or by time's, she does not know. They shield from her the context of their lives between-times; she is just a womb, she is little more than a machine, she has no purpose for them beyond reproduction. Perhaps they are afraid of her, for all that each time they overpower her; but if they do fear her, this does not assist her, nothing assists her against them, they are always too many.

But now there are only three of the daughter-selves, and they all akin to a mirror image of her; now there are two, and both seemingly older than her their mother; now there is but one, for one of the twins has died, and this other, this survivor, is elderly and lonely.

This other, the frail old daughter, she has a name, and the name has been told; but why should she, the mother, have any need of this name from one who effectively kept her imprisoned? Why should she accede, in any fashion, to this last representative of those who oppressed her? Why should she stay warm, now, for another's need for company, when her own needs have always been rendered subservient to those of her descendants? Why should she not, now, simply radiate the cold in which they so repeatedly insisted she should remain stowed? This is her nature, after all; this is the role they have required of her.

But it is difficult to be human, and to remain frozen: it can be done, for a time, but the cost accumulates.

Merieka gives her time, gives her space, the younger one, the mother; there's nothing else Drusil wants, not conversation, not company, not comfort, not even food in those first days out of cryo. Merieka doesn't fully understand, though she recognizes the needs of anger and is prepared to wait those out, for what else can she do? Merieka's is not a position from which she can negotiate cleanly: she was never a ringleader, nor can she claim blamelessness. She was simply one of the group, hiding first behind her youth and then, when that leached out, behind her passivity. She has always been the sort to let others take the lead and the risks. This might, in truth, be what she is still doing now, might indeed be why in her ninetieth year she is still alive, but it does not assist her to explore the notion; no, she will simply wait, and if waiting is not enough then waiting is not enough. She knows that what they did to Drusil was utterly unfair; and yet what choice existed, given their predicament? Without those actions their group would have died out a century ago, or more, two centuries, three, back almost to the era when there were still men as well as women, before the contagion that blighted maleness; and Merieka herself would now be as dead as the rest, or would never have been.

It's not as though attempts were not made—wide-ranging and thorough attempts, across the many years while the group lingered and dwindled—to understand the mechanism by which Drusil, and Drusil alone among her line, was able (is able) to reproduce, complete and unassisted. Biopsies carefully taken from the ice-enshrouded woman had established that the mechanism was not a matter of genetics, for there have been daughters who carry all her genes, nor does it appear to reside in bodily structure, since here too the mother is not unique. There is instead something ineffable, inscrutable, which has enabled for her the trick of parthenogenesis; they've tried to understand it, but they cannot.

Merieka's dilemma is this: because her guilt is not the whole guilt, she holds back, holds off, is not sure of the nuance. Or at least her mind is not sure; her body is content to accumulate stress, to pool it in her gut and to yoke it across her shoulders, and so for days, a month, she lives with the ache of it, the gripe, tends to the hydroponics and the life-support controllers and all of the other apparatuses which are able to maintain themselves in any event; but she must keep herself busy until she is fully ready to take on all the responsibility for the actions of others, and to apologize, awkwardly, messily, completely to Drusil. It does not help—that is, it appears not to help—and yet two days later Drusil finally responds to her, in a voice so ill-used as to scarce seem human still, and to ask her, angrily and without grace, what is her name again. They proceed, flintily and with much misunderstanding, to converse, and these times for Merieka are more difficult than the weeks of frozen silence, for now the cost of failure has been sharpened. She has connected with Drusil, at last, but their shared existence has grown more brittle as the ice crust has thawed. It is not until they learn that Drusil has once again fallen pregnant to herself that the bond between them becomes something strong enough to bear weight. Those last two years, for Merieka, are good ones, cleansing, close, a calm end to an often-difficult and narrow life. She finds, at the end, a friendship with Drusil, finds the companionship she had sought: not delivered in response to the demand which she passively placed upon the mother, but offered to her as a gift. Even when Merieka grows enfeebled beyond the capabilities of medical intervention, there are compensations to ease her looming death. The child, her nine-decades-younger sister, means she will not be leaving Drusil to solitude.

The fate the child will face, when Drusil herself ultimately passes, is not Merieka's concern.

It's Drusil's concern, though. Her daughter Agnete, whom she not only births but mothers—her first opportunity to do so, because there are no longer the numbers to stop her—will have a lonely life and an empty one unless Drusil does as she has always done before, which is to bear her a sibling. But now, when it matters, when it matters to *her* rather than to this nebulous conceptualisation of 'the settlement', it does not happen. Agnete grows, two years, five years, and still there is no younger sister. When Agnete turns seven, Drusil accepts what has become increasingly apparent: that the marvellous machinery of her, this life-giving force within her, has worn out. Agnete's the last.

Drusil plans for this, and she waits. Researches and waits. Argues desperately with herself and waits. Sees to the settlement's maintenance, checks and rechecks all the power feeds and air purification systems and nutrient bioreactors and waits. Teaches all of this, also, in detail and with patience, to her young and growing daughter and waits. In personality, Agnete becomes—and how could it be otherwise?—a younger version of Drusil herself. Serious, stubborn, careful, quiet. The girl grows. Drusil strives to conceal her own anxiety, because there is still a chance, a small one, that what was kindled in her, this metabolic talent for parthenogenesis, will spark in Agnete also.

It does not. Agnete turns sixteen, turns eighteen by the calendar, and it has not happened. Drusil herself was twice a mother by this point, or so she thinks; it's difficult to be sure of the chronology, with ninety percent of her existence submerged and icebound from that point until Agnete's birth. Drusil must accept, now—and she has reached an age where acceptance comes more easily somehow, with less fanfare and less internal argument—that Agnete won't bear herself any children. So Drusil prepares a sedative. She'll spare her daughter the decades of isolation.

Agnete discovers her mother's intentions, confronts her, calls her out. It transpires that Agnete is not simply a duplicate of her mother, she has acquired a pugnacity and a fierceness which she now brings to bear (verbally; there is no need for physical dominance, for Drusil is old) in adamantly resisting this ploy.

Drusil argues that Agnete is condemning herself to decades alone. Agnete responds that she does not care, she doesn't wish to be frozen. Drusil attempts to tell her daughter that Agnete does not know what solitude is, and Agnete answers, with a turn of phrase clearly designed to sting, that she indeed knows solitude very well, is intimately acquainted. It escalates from there, and the two do not communicate for several days.

When contact is finally reestablished, it's at Agnete's hand, and the olive branch she bears is nonetheless barbed. *I don't want to outlive you,* she tells her mother. *If you're the one frozen, I won't have to; I'll merely be waiting several decades to see you again. I can do that, if you can do that.*

It's a good argument, and Agnete is stronger than her mother in several respects.

Agnete tends methodically to the settlement's maintenance, pays particular heed to the power feed for the cryosuspension pod, and waits. It's supremely quiet.

THE FIRST TEN MULTIPLES OF 18

(RANKED ON AESTHETIC GROUNDS FROM WORST TO BEST)

10th: 54.

It's churlish to deride an essentially blameless number, but this isn't what's happening here. 54 is a rubbish multiple of 18. It's obvious that there's an 18-multiple somewhere in the 50s, but is it 54? or 56? or maybe 52? Nobody knows. Useless. Get in the bin, 54.

9th: 126.

This at least has the excuse that it edges into three figures, but it's still far too obscure to constitute a decent multiple of 18. Weak.

8th: 162.

Wins out over 126 on two grounds: (1) it's slightly larger, and (2) it can be obtained by subtracting one clear multiple of 18 (18 itself) from another (180). Still a very shabby multiple for all that. Do better, 162.

7th: 90.

Far too bloody sure of itself, and what has it ever achieved? An utter grifter of a multiple.

6th: 18.

Yes, you're a multiple of yourself. Big whoop. Way to go, Captain Obvious.

5th: 144.

This should be much better known as a multiple of 18, but it's so lah-de-dah about being the square of 12 that nobody can be bothered remembering the 18 connection. If it isn't a disappointment to its parents, it deserves to be.

4th: 180.

Speaking of Captain Obvious…

3rd: 36.

Could possibly have snagged the top spot, but it's just that little bit inconsequential. Also another square, and you can never really trust those.

2nd: 108.

Now we're getting somewhere. This one is just that slight bit mysterious, but combine that with the fact that it's an anagram of another multiple (the halfway-decent 180), and you end up with something pretty classy. Nice.

1st: 72.

You know it makes sense.

THE LIFE CHOICES OF PI

The millionth digit of pi booked a holiday.

Now this simple eight-word, twelve-syllable statement, unremarkable in several ways, provokes many questions. The least important of those questions is 'so what actually is pi's millionth digit?' In fact, I'm slightly ashamed of you for even considering it, or of myself for imagining that you are or were considering it, whether or not you are or were, because it's not at all relevant to the story, which is to say I've no idea what that digit is, and why should I? What purpose, really, does the millionth digit of pi serve? Nothing in the observable universe is remotely that perfectly round so as to require accuracy expressed to such a digit, not the roundest ever orange, not the horizon, not Michelangelo's best freehand circle, not the world's most expensive precision-machined pizza cutter, not even an atom. The millionth digit of pi does nothing for no-one, except perhaps for mathematical fetishists, of whom I can assure you I'm not one.

So, the millionth digit of pi: pointless, in essence. Without any significant value. And the digit itself surely knew this, could see at first hand its own lack of any meaningful contribution to circularity, to sphericity, to the phenomenon of curvature in general, which we must presume is why it had booked the holiday.

Let's look more closely at its motivation. The millionth digit was not a religious digit in any sense, but it recognised that any entity, even a number, ought to have a soul of sorts, or at least a personality of sorts, or at least a nature that was more than just the sum of its parts. But did it? For itself, it couldn't truthfully answer yes or no. The millionth digit needed time and space in which to re-evaluate its personal circumstances, and it was not going to get that time and space jostled in the queue between digit nine hundred and ninety-nine thousand, nine hundred and ninety-nine and digit one million and one. And while it was apparently true that none of the unimaginably numberless sequence of digits of pi had ever taken a holiday before this, who—other than the aforementioned mathematical fetishists— would ever notice? Oranges wouldn't buckle. Cathedral domes wouldn't collapse in on themselves. None of the sixteen billion human eyes observing their next sunset would perceive any aberrance whatsoever in that radiant globe's setting, compared to the previous sunsets those eight billion humans had seen.

This, all up, is rather more verbiage than I had intended to waste on that least important question, and it's meant I don't have as much space to properly address any of the more relevant ones: would it journey by train, by boat, by aircraft? Would it, perhaps, walk? Could it, indeed, walk? What form would the holiday take? Where would it go? Would it need to dress for the expected weather at its intended destination? What would an arbitrary digit look like in swimwear, in skiwear, in evening wear? For how long would it be away? Had it asked anyone to mind its place while it was gone?

By air, perhaps, naturally yes, a round-the-world trip (because of course), it didn't know, that sounded sensible, that's none of your business quite frankly, it hadn't decided, and no.

In fact, it didn't go famously, not by a long stretch. The millionth digit of pi missed its flight, failed to book a replacement flight, and ended up getting hopelessly drunk in a series of bars in the airport's vicinity, from which it was sequentially thrown out for disorderly conduct. It passed out, woke up the next morning to find itself in unfamiliar lodgings, sharing a dishevelled bed with a hirsute complex number which it had no recollection of meeting and which smelled, frankly, of cigarette smoke, mould-raddled garlic, and diseased piss. Sordid and disconnected images gradually revealed themselves to the millionth digit, unveiling the extent of the previous night's depravity (in which it had been an all-too-willing participant, with regard to an attempted hold-up of an all-night convenience store, for cigarettes and pictorial adult literature; with regard to an all-in brawl with nightclub bouncers, where it had found itself quantifiably outnumbered; and with regard, most shamefully, to repeated episodes of karaoke), while it now lay there, whimpering as quietly as possible, wretchedly regretting its dubious actions and hoping it could make its escape without waking its seedy and apparently flatulent complex-number bedfellow, because that was a conversation it really did not wish to have. It had always been, in these matters, a strictly real-number sort of digit, and now this. It was too much.

Hungover and nauseous, it fled. It took itself home. Which is to say, it went back to its place in the familiar sequence of pi. But it requires focus, patience, and a clear head to count to exactly one million, which is to say that the millionth digit badly miscounted and intercalated itself between two completely incorrect, though numerically familiar, digits in the sequence, because after all there are many, many such combinations along the myriad digits of pi. Its misplacement was far enough along that the orange-fanciers would never notice the infinitesimal change in pi's value, far enough along that the sunset and the horizon would not be in any way changed for any observers, nor any atoms implode or explode as a consequence of the shift, far enough along that the pizza wheels would still roll as perfectly as ever they had, far enough indeed that only the mathematical fetishists would be outraged by this disturbance in the natural order—not that you, I hope, are sufficiently naïve to pay any attention to the mathematical fetishists' witterings. Had anybody learnt anything from all this?

No, except possibly for the former millionth digit of pi, which now had less idea than ever as to what its role was in all these things.

Which is perhaps as it should be, because sometimes there doesn't have to be a role.

ATOM

He was a strange one, was Atom, who could see clearly only in near or full darkness. Light fogged his vision, the brighter the murkier.

He was born thus, though neither he nor his parents knew this at first. They thought him blind, this infant who usually failed to make proper eye contact, who did not respond to gestures made or faces pulled in bright-lit rooms, who was fearful of sunlit exterior spaces. A blind boy, who would not sleep in a darkened room. (And why would he? It was only then that he saw the toys in his bedroom, or the furniture, or the wallpaper, or the drapes which stretched across the windows; only then he truly saw his parents as anything more than a dull blur. In darkness, he was overstimulated for the purposes of sleep.)

He was a boy alone; he would not play with other children, or perhaps it was truer that they would not play with him, this child who seemingly could not catch, this child whom sunlight made torpid, this child who, when he was old enough, would hide things in cupboards, would hide himself in those cupboards so he could inspect his prizes. And still they all thought him blind, his family and the nurses and the other families with children with whom his parents associated. It was thus they began to teach him braille, because his parents felt strongly that he should not be disadvantaged when it came time for school to take him.

He learnt the braille, the rudiments at least, the bumps which spelled his name, Atom.

How did his parents learn he had darksight? Most likely it would have been when he was three or four, and was found shut in a wardrobe, perusing a picture book. In the darkness.

This was not straightforward blindness, it was clear; and his parents were, at first, alarmed: they had not expected of their child this behaviour, this ability. It was a complication they did not need, but of course all parents face complications in some form, as their children learn and grow and change. In another century or another place they might have deemed it witchcraft, or demonic possession, or a sickness, or some other suggestion that the unusual was aberrant. Atom's parents sought medical help, which resulted in a long series of tests and scans and consultations.

If the parents were hoping for an explanation, or perhaps even a cure, which one must suppose they were, then the medical inquisitions did not deliver this. The boy could see in darkness, could see best in perfect darkness, could see only under conditions at least approximating to darkness. This couldn't be accounted for in a genetic manner, or on the basis of anatomy; there was no mutation responsible for what his parents saw as their son's 'condition'; nor could optics account for it, for all that it behaved like a more or less straightforward inversion of standard optical properties. When the specialists had exhausted their repertoires and their imaginations, the parents were told they just must needs accept it. Which, by and large, they did. Atom would be content, by and large, if they were content with Atom. Which they were, or tried to be. By and large.

Others were not. There were family friends who refused to let their children play with 'that strange wrongly-blind boy'; there were others who were happy enough to let their children visit

Atom's house, but who would not host him at their own home because they did not feel that they could provide for his needs. Gradually the family nucleated around a group who just accepted him (and in some cases did so more easily and less awkwardly than did Atom's parents themselves, at times, for a child who sees 'lights out' as an invitation to get up and explore is not an easy child to have in the house).

Atom was by nature nocturnal, which is perhaps no surprise but which his parents saw as problematic: his socialisation would suffer if he was mainly awake when most were asleep. A shuttered window, roller blinds and blackout curtains in Atom's room provided a solution, augmented by a policy of lights-on at bedtime. Thus was he coaxed, over several weeks, into a circadian rhythm largely in keeping with most of his peers.

He was home-schooled, obviously, because there are some scenarios with which the public education system is simply not equipped to deal.

He was solitary by nature, obviously.

He was aware, obviously, that he was very different to other children in his circle. Sometimes the knowledge of this hurt him deeply, caused him to question who he was.

He was who he was.

He grew into adulthood.

There was a knock at his door. 'Wait,' Atom called, and busied himself with finding and lighting the tealights, the localised burst of black as the match struck, the larger blob of darkness as the inky flame burgeoned at the wick's top. Three candles were the compromise he'd reached with the wider world: with three candles spaced around the room, each person saw a dim scene, while nobody was confronted by full darkness.

He could've achieved the same effect with a couple of very low-luminosity electric bulbs, suitably shaded, but he liked the sharp sweet smell of molten paraffin. It awoke associations in him.

He opened the door. Too bright: the streetlight across the road, a glare of all-consuming black. He couldn't see.

'It's Marilyn,' she said, and it took him a few seconds to remember which one was Marilyn, from the lecture class he attended remotely.

'Hi,' he replied, stepping back from the door.

'May I come in?'

'Sure.'

She closed the door behind her, and the ink faded: now he could see her. She wasn't as he'd imagined; she was taller, stockier, with a hare lip and a reedy voice which sounded as though it belonged to someone thinner. Hair might have been blue, might have been green: he wasn't sure which yet. She was pretty, and he had no idea why she was here.

She was carrying a medium-sized daypack by its handle: it, too, might have been blue, might have been green.

'Would you like some water? Tea?'

'I'm fine.' She was staring at him, as though she also had never seen him before; but that couldn't be right, he sometimes turned his camera on as a courtesy. 'It got me thinking, that thing you said last week, about never having seen a movie or a program on TV. I thought we could do something about that. If it wouldn't be keeping you from somewhere else.'

'It's very generous of you. But they don't make movies that I could ever watch.'

'I got that. But I can give you a play-by-play.'

'I wouldn't even know how to set one up on the computer, I haven't used the voice activation for anything like that.'

'That's fine,' she said. 'I've got the gear.'

'It's really not necessary,' he said, attempting to marshal his wits. Except for family, people didn't visit, for obvious reasons; and he was out of practice at conversing like this, with no time for forethought. Though probably, he couldn't help thinking, she'd had such time, she must have, in planning to drop in. The thought irked him, and it irked him that it irked him. It was trouble enough being a loner; he didn't want to get tagged with the 'curmudgeon' label too. 'I can access any book I wish, all the music, radio drama, I could do art galleries and sculpture if they'd turn the lights out once every so often. I really don't need movies or TV, I don't feel that I'm missing out on anything.'

'I'd say you are,' said Marilyn. She gestured to the table and chairs. 'May we sit down?'

'I guess.' They did so. Her hair was green, he could see that now. He realised he'd been hoping it would be blue. 'Why do you say I'm missing something?'

'Books don't give you the dance of human interaction: they can describe events, but they are only conveying that indirectly, with words. They're always tell, not show. Radio dramas don't give you the physicality, the body language, any of that stuff. Video gives you scenes in which you can see things play out. It's not life, but it's a portrayal of life. There isn't anything quite like it.'

'Great, so you're telling me I'm missing out on something after all.'

'No. Well, yes, in a sense, but we can do something about that.'

'I don't see what. I've tried watching TV shows before. It's just dark, and the sound quality usually isn't clear enough to provide context. If I want live-action, radio does it better.'

'We can fix that. Well, not the sound, but the vision.'

'We?'

'My boyfriend's in signals processing.'

He filed the information in his memory, aware of a mild disappointment. 'So how does this work? A simple negative image won't cut it. What I see—with radiant light, the brilliance is inverted, but the colours aren't. Or actually, who knows? My red might be utterly different to yours. It's still red, though. I think.'

'Give me five minutes to set up,' she said, bending down to retrieve a laptop from her daypack. 'You'll probably want to douse those candles, there'll be enough illumination onscreen, and it'll be simpler if there are no competing sources. Then we'll see what we can see.'

'So assuming this works, what do you have for me to watch?'

'An absolute classic,' she said, and would not be drawn further. 'Hush now. This might take a little experimentation until we get the settings right for you.'

Afterwards, he felt— well, he wasn't sure, or maybe it was that he didn't trust himself to try to find words. But clearly it was necessary to say *something*. 'Thank you.'

'You're welcome,' she replied, and there was something a little too ingratiating about her smile, as though she knew she'd won a bet, or that he'd lost one. 'From a technical sense, a visual sense, did that work for you?'

'Pretty much. The colours were right, I think, but they were slightly muted, not like what I'd see in what you call full darkness. But that was maybe just that video. They weren't all vivid colour, were they?'

'That one's fairly vivid. We can fine-tune that, heighten the colour contrast.'

'That'd make it look strange to you, wouldn't it? I know your eyes work differently to mine.'

'That doesn't bother me.' She made eye contact, her pupils wide in the gloom cast by the laptop's screen. 'Would you still say you haven't been missing out on anything?'

'I need to think about that. And yes, it was very … immersive, in a way. I liked the story. It wasn't what I was expecting, but I can see why you called it a classic. Thank you.'

'You're welcome,' she said again. 'So you enjoyed the show? I was worried it might not have been a good starting point, there are a lot of references to other movies and shows you wouldn't have twigged to.'

'That didn't bother me,' he replied. 'But I suppose I just didn't see what Gromit saw in that woman he fell in love with.'

'Gromit was the dog, the clever one,' she said. 'The guy you're thinking of was Wallace.'

'And are they all like that, these movies?'

'Oh, no,' she said, and laughed. 'I'll have that tea, now, if you're still offering.'

He served her the tea, noticed as she picked it up that there was a bruise on the side of her wrist. He didn't know her well enough to ask, and it wasn't his business anyway.

The video evenings became a fortnightly fixture. At first Atom found them intrusive; he was used to his own time, and there was after all something quite artificial about these onscreen images—they didn't allow you your own pace, they didn't invite you to pause and pick them up later. Or perhaps it was that they weren't a solitary thing; it was like two people reading the same book at the same time, which felt odd. He mentioned this to Marilyn, on the second or maybe the third evening. Couldn't this overlay, after all, this signal-processing adaptation of the video player, couldn't this be downloaded onto his own computer, and not just kept on her laptop?

'It's still under development,' she explained. 'In time, yes, there'll be a copy for you. But there are still some technical tradeoffs that my— that we're working through.'

They watched *Whale Rider. Casablanca. Little Miss Sunshine.* Each one stranger in its way than the one before. Gradually he allowed that he might be developing a taste for this artform. *Alien. Titanic. The Big Sleep.* He found himself wondering what Marilyn did those other thirteen evenings a fortnight, but he supposed there really wasn't any mystery there. *Stalker. The Gold Rush. North By Northwest.* It was good, actually. He started to read up, and to put in his own requests for the next time. They weren't all available, but he felt that his part in the process was no longer merely passive.

The knock at the door. He was puzzled: Thursday, yes, but this was an off week—

He opened the door. The streetlight, blinding, but this was a closer darkness, deeper than that, a flashlight flaring full-face.

A hand on his chest, shoving hard. He stumbled back, turning to escape the flashlight's inky beam. There was a chair, he didn't see it, his shin found it. He fell, moving his arms to cushion himself against the table, which he knew to be there. The door slammed shut.

He dodged the table, but the attacker had followed him in. Rasping breaths, a sharp solid blow to his chest, another to his stomach. He sought to defend his torso against the kicks. The kicks bypassed his defences, landed harder. It wasn't safe to breathe, or maybe it wasn't possible. A particularly solid kick to his groin. Then a pause. The sound of a chair scraped to one side. The assailant moved closer, Atom could hear the rasping breaths nearing the floor. The torch-beam, intense and opaque, full in his face.

'You'll keep away from her.' A male voice, deep, delivered slow and with venom. Then the man stood; the chair-scrape once again; the darkness still full-face. The door opened, closed. The ink ebbed slowly, as Atom tested to find out where it hurt most. He stood, hobbled to the door, ensured it was properly locked. He moved cautiously to the bathroom, in case he needed to throw up. Ran a bath.

*

Another Thursday. A knock at the door; his heartrate ramped reflexively. He checked the peephole, apprehensive. She'd pressed her face close, framed it by overarching hands so he didn't just see darkness. 'Please go away,' he said, wondering why the words hurt so much.

'Atom, I—'

'I can't do this,' he told her.

'I've left him,' she replied, her voice still muffled by the door.

'You think that makes me safer?' he asked, and belatedly, eye to the door's peephole, he saw the condition of her face. He felt awful then; opened the door; stepped back.

She came in, hugged him as the door swung closed behind her. They'd never touched, and this hurt too.

He stepped back again. 'I'm sorry,' he said, eyeing the bruised side of her face.

'You're not the one who should be apologising,' she told him. 'I'm the one who knew what Tate was like. But I didn't think he'd be like that with someone else.'

He found matches, lit a candle. Sacrificing perfect clarity so she didn't need to contend with darkness. 'Let's go sit down,' he said, gesturing to the table and chairs.

She took off her daypack, pulled a chair back. 'I'd like tea, if you're offering.' There was silence a minute, while he busied himself with the jug and the cups. 'It must've hurt. I'm sorry to have brought it on you.'

'You were trying to do a good thing,' he said, sitting down, sliding her cup across to her. 'You *were* doing a good thing. He— yes, it hurt. There are still a few reminders. The way he went about it, the flashlight in my face, he'd obviously planned it out. And I'm buggered if those weren't steel-cap boots.'

She reached a hand toward his, reconsidered, withdrew. Touched the bruised side of her face. 'He's out of action for the next four months or so, for what that's worth.'

He shrugged. 'I get the sense you didn't just pop round to apologise. Or for the budget-brand bag tea.'

'No,' she said. 'This is a farewell.'

There was plainly more; he waited.

'I'm moving interstate next week. I've been taken on by that university. It's too good an opportunity to pass up.'

'Congratulations,' he said, taking care to keep his voice level. 'I hope it works out well.'

'And I have something for you.' She took a thumb drive from her pocket. 'You'll need to get your own laptop. I thought we should watch this one on yours. If you don't have other plans for the evening.'

He laughed ruefully. 'I never have other plans. But—my laptop? I thought you were still refining the code.'

She touched her cheek again. 'It's as finished as it's going to get.'

The installation took a couple of minutes, then she went over the settings with him, helped him interface it with the voice-command software. 'I think we're set,' she announced.

'So what did you have planned for this evening's viewing?'

'Something short and sweet. Something that closes the cycle.' She retrieved a brightly coloured DVD case from her daypack. 'Does the name Feathers McGraw mean anything to you?'

They sat on his sofa, perched his laptop on a kitchen chair in front of them. Partway through the show, her hand found his, and stayed there. That was as far as it went.

The following days felt empty, but life progressed. There were never any knocks at the door that were not the pre-arranged visits from one or other parent, or simple deliveries.

One morning, about a year later, there was a delivery he hadn't ordered, but which he needed to sign for nonetheless. A small carton, solidly wrapped in parcel tape. Too big to be a fountain pen, the wrong shape for a book. He couldn't read the sender's address until he took it inside.

He found scissors to carefully slice through all the tape. The box fell open; a spillage of packing peanuts onto the table. A handwritten note and a pair of spectacles. He read the note through twice. It was brief, and most of it was technical, but the last paragraph was personal and gave him more hope than perhaps it should have.

The spectacles were dark-lensed, heavy, very chunky. There were a few small switches and controls built into the right arm. A tag, loosely tied by ribbon to the left arm, the same handwriting: *Think of me when you wear these.*

He set the controls as the note suggested, slipped the glasses on. Parted the curtains and rolled up the blinds, waited for an inky sightlessness that didn't eventuate. There was a delay of a second or so in the image processing, but he figured that would be ok if he didn't move too fast.

He checked his clothes were tidy and his fly fastened, then he ventured outside, looked up into sunshine. He'd have to write and tell her this: that there were actual clouds in the actual sky.

MILQUETOAST

Milquetoast was your standard everyday common-or-garden hero. He'd slain an utterly run-of-the-mill monster using typically mundane weaponry which wasn't really up to the task, but he'd relied on the usual guile and a modicum of inventive thinking to get the deed done and, as generally happened, had emerged victorious from the fray. There'd been a generic and indifferently catered celebration in his honour, where the townsfolk showered him with mediocre gratitude, and he supposed he should've been happy with that. But he wasn't happy, not one bit: Milquetoast wanted more.

He couldn't *handle* more, but he didn't know that yet.

ARTHOUSE

None of this happened, and it happened in this particular order: a sunset, smeared pale across the western rim | a face, neither yours nor mine nor anyone known to either of us | the cat's cry, directly above | a solar eclipse, unexpectedly followed twelve minutes later by a second solar eclipse as the moon changes tack | a vain effort to quench the arterial bleeding by force of will alone | a powerful person quietly saying they understand now, and are truly sorry | the leaf litter, ubiquitous throughout the derelict hotel | a building site, the work long abandoned due to a funding dispute | the new number's discovery, promoting great excitement among the mathematicians | the tick, tick, tick of the injured patient's clockwork heart | the child's distress at having wandered too far | the fifty-five Hertz hiss, growing louder as the vision fades | the other things, also, not listed here separately | those words which you said you said to me | the flowers' dread of the florist's blade | corrosion of the facial recognition training set by inclusion of images of hand-puppets | the jacket, lost, the argument, lost, the traveller, lost, the time, lost | the sudden change of mind by the bride-to-be | joyriders, laughing loud in the moments before the crash | one passerby waving to another, thinking they once knew someone who owned such a jacket | the adulterers arranging to meet in a large Central European railway station, variously Bucharest or Budapest / the protagonist's soliloquy, lacking rhyme, coherence, or consistent meter / the flame, strengthening quickly as it climbs the curtain / the masked criminal, apprehended only because his hand-puppet is recognised / the funeral's solemnity / the novelty supply factory worker, drowned in a vat of fake blood / belated realisation that all of the above is just the trailer.

ALLSHIP

The air is acceptable, the gravity's comfortable, water's always water. But the bread isn't bread, the milk isn't milk, the fruit's not fruit. There's no purpose bewailing any of this, it is just the way of it here. We chose this; those of us who are here chose this.

The coffee's still coffee, because humans insist on it.

Our contribution to galactic culture: caffeine.

There are few takers for it among the others.

We have to stop this, I say. It can't go on. *I* can't go on. I can't keep doing this. It needs to stop.

All this I say, while I'm alone at the table, alone in the human foodhall. The others are off at some event. I'm here rehearsing. Playing with my food of unknown provenance, while I prep for this morning's two committee meetings.

We'd thought humanity alone across the swathe. Hundreds of billions of star systems, utterly vacant, all awaiting Earthlife's expansion. We were mistaken.

We'd thought lightspeed the limit, inviolable; but there appear to be shortcuts.

We'd thought that, in the unlikely circumstance there were other technologically advanced civilisations within the Galaxy, there'd be the prospect of war as a means of resolving resource competition. It turns out we were wrong there too.

Such questions across the Galaxy are addressed not through combat, but through structured dialogue between species, which is arguably more brutal and in some respects more final.

I'm sorry, I say. I was staring, that's rude.

They don't reply straightaway. When they do, there's a further several-second pause before their translator sounds. Maybe that's standard with bronter syntax, I wouldn't know. *Rude is like a transgression of etiquette, isn't it? I didn't perceive a breach.*

The translator's voice is somewhere in the uneasy territory between organic and mechanical. Male-leaning. Probably this one hasn't communicated much with humans before, their device still on default. I raise my eyes from my drink, chance another perusal of the scarring on their dermis: it's easier than looking at that maw, those eyes, that snout. That broad visage, that utter lack of neck. The exaggerated musculature around the creature's mouth, and what that implies. The flank's scarring doesn't look fresh, but what do I know, beyond the absolute basics, of their metabolism? I'm diplomacy, not xenozoology. A junior advisor, who will likely have a larger role only if things go bad.

(Caal has told me there's no chance that things will go bad. I believed him, once, and of course I found his confidence attractive.)

Have you produced children recently? I ask the bronter, glancing again at the scars and marveling at my own impertinence.

Again the delay, as we would assess it, before the response. *Recently? No. But I have generated offspring, several times, the youngest of them numerous years ago as your kind would reckon it.* They lean forward, reach with a prehensile-looking tongue to sample their own drink, a putrid and viscous brew in a broad-mouthed brushed metal canister; I'm nursing my own drink in my hands, so as to better protect it from contact with that tongue, and with whatever it is the bronter is imbibing. They close first one eye and then the other two, in what I am starting to interpret as a gesture of momentary relaxation.

I thought they grew back after, I say. The arms.

Often. Not always. Something interesting has happened: the translating device's voice is now coded more closely to my own. This change in response, after so little dialogue, almost certainly means this bronter's equipment—and by extension, the bronter themself—has had very little prior contact with humans. So I'll need to be careful to not cause offence. But I also need to know whether this one's loss of their breeding arms is a problem, in terms of status: it's important to understand, as we pursue the formal dialogue elsewhere within the ship, where this one fits in the pecking order. Their presence here, aboard the ship currently transiting subspace, argues they have some cachet at least, but these things are always relative. For example, I'm here also.

Still, it could be useful to cultivate this bronter's acquaintance; it could equally well be counterproductive. So much depends on standing.

Is that a loss? I ask. A loss of self, I mean, not merely of appendages. Or does the... reproductive achievement outweigh that?

I don't understand the question.

I didn't express it well. It's a difficult concept for humans to grasp, I think. This idea that your species can reproduce by shedding limbs. By consuming the severed limbs of others of your kind. It's so... *alien*, I manage to curb myself from saying.

The voice now granite, warmer, androgyne. *The limbs, the maw-pouch, are where the generative tissue is. And it's not just 'our species'. All the fauna of our world do this, it's normal. I could equally say that it's difficult for us to understand the conjoining process which your species practises, your phylum practises, if I understand correctly. This perversion, if I may call it that, of your phylum's excretory functions to accommodate also your reproductive capacity; there seems nothing natural about that. How does it work, that you couple in this way, without the necessity of contest? Are you not territorial beings? Surely you must be, else you would not be aboard.*

I stare at their hide a few moments, waiting to find a way to respond. Feeling lost, and wondering whether it's the alcohol that's at fault, or an insufficiency of same. This strange tasteless liquid, a small tumbler: water with more kick than vodka. This foothill of flesh, of teeth, the rheumy ellipsis of its gaze… We are territorial beings, yes. But social also.

Social does not sit with us. When I meet another, we fight. Territory must be defended. Young are prey. Not those who carry my scent, my offspring. Those I don't eat. This notion of grouping with others of your kind: it's very strange. They lift the canister towards their maw; the tongue need not reach so far to take its sample. They close one eye, then the other two. *For my part, I don't understand how such a war-hungry species as yours can coexist in such numbers, can seek consensus among yourselves. Am I right in understanding you still fight amongst yourselves, organised combat between large groupings arranged by geography or ideology? We have nothing like that, never have; we could not. Murder, yes, as you would term it: one of us may kill another, for territorial advantage or to avenge the death of a brood of young, but not such organisation nor such discipline as I've heard you apply to the task of war. Have you slain many yourself, of your kind?*

None.

Then am I mistaken? As I understand it, your kind venerates the most effective warriors among you. I would have expected such to populate your negotiation team here. Are you therefore low-caste?

No, I tell them. 'Warrior' is a specialisation; our society has many specialisations. Mine is negotiation.

How strange. They close one eye, then two. I suppose then we would have to describe ourselves as generalists, each a society unto themself. It's necessary that it's so, for us. We keep ourselves few, which you do not. If I might make a pointed observation?

Please do.

I think you will find yourself at a disadvantage, here, in these negotiations. We would like another world, this we freely admit. But you need another one, because you are poisoning the one you have. It's not a strong bargaining position.

I think you're incorrect to say we're poisoning the Earth. I will concede there are difficulties in resourcing, but—

Is it not true that you eat all life, on your world? To the point of extinction of many species? We who you see as murderous barbarian hermits—and I have read the reports of your kind which state as much— we do not dominate the life on our world. We have some influence over it, yes, but we are not like you, we do not control it. We choose not to, and in fact we would not be able to, we cannot coexist in the numbers that would be required, for us to overrun our world. We have the discipline you lack.

I've vowed I wouldn't visit Caal; this was the entire purpose, after all, of spending time in the multispecies sector, where I know he never goes. But the alcohol suggests otherwise, and the dialogue with the bronter — the all too frequent alien obsession with the mechanics of copulation — has sparked a certain drive.

If he's surprised to see me, at such a late hour, he doesn't display it. He lets me in, offers a seat, we talk.

We're very different, Caal and I: there's a vitality to him, an enthusiasm, a lack of caution. Sometimes it's infectious. On this occasion, not; but I'd rather not do this alone, and in the moment, there's no impediment. It's just the simplest way, a bad habit of mine.

When the discussion has reached that point, without ever having directly touched upon it, we move through to the bedroom.

We touch. We draw closer. We kick things off, down a familiar track.

Things progress as expected, going well—almost there for me, with Caal, under me, not far behind I think—when he grips my arm, hard: urgency, agency. I picture the bronter, watching. My arms, attached, vulnerable. I lose the rhythm, slump to a halt. Caal pushes up into me twice, thrice more, he's keen to press on, but it's stopped working for me, and now for him too. Those eyes, that maw. I slide off, lie down at Caal's side: the heat of him, the sweat, his and mine both, the breaths, his and mine both, the goal not reached. He doesn't understand, and how could he? I'm not sure myself. I kiss his stubbled cheek, he mumbles something I don't catch.

His arm against my chest; I reposition slightly, to break that contact. Those eyes, that maw: the force required to wrench that arm off. I'm very protective, suddenly, of my shoulders.

Sorry, I say. I just can't.

Time to go. I get up.

Alcohol, lateness of hour, an unsettled mental state, the thing which just happened; I know not to send, in such circumstances. But send I do: I can't keep doing this.

My implant registers the response ten minutes later, as I'm in my quarters and preparing for sleep: Do you mean the negotiations?

He knows I don't mean that. Let him sweat, I tell myself, and refrain from replying.

It's a poor sleep; the alcohol isn't to blame, not really.

I'm still mulling over the bronter's words as I prepare, at the next daycycle's start, for our team's strategy session. For obvious reasons, fatigued and frazzled, it's not a meeting I'm looking forward to.

Mars, the bronter had said, just before I'd taken my leave. *Mars is what we want. There would be space there for another ten thousand of us, once the environment had been prepared. We could never endure on your Earth, our own weight would crush us. But Mars is perfect for our needs, more as I understand it than for yours. The world we will provide you in exchange would surely be fair recompense: larger, naturally verdant, welcoming for your kind.*

I can't keep doing this. My mantra, my safe words. I repeat the words, to myself only, as I find a seat for myself; don't meet his gaze, his unasked query. He won't start anything, in public here, not with eight or nine others present, two of them senior to himself; and I know to not keep my implant active. Let him sweat. He knows my meaning, in any case, if not precisely my reasons.

Whatever we expected contact to be, whatever we had expected to be the results of our intentional and inadvertent broadcasts to the galaxy, it wasn't this. They all knew each other.

They all knew each other. Was that so surprising? It should not have been, we were the latecomers; they'd had aeons. But: they all knew each other and they all travelled together.

Could we trust them? No; we didn't know them. We'd had no inkling. But: they all knew each other, they all travelled together, and they bade us join them. On this vast ship.

We'd workshopped many scenarios, but never this. Refusal's consequences were unknowable, and this was clearly a highly diverse grouping, suggesting an overview of mutual acceptance or at least tolerance; we cautiously assented.

The idea of the ship: it was a government, a parliament, a meeting place, a place of introduction, of negotiation, of collaboration. It was all these things, more or less: a bureaucracy, though its operations were not directed from above, so far as we could establish. One of my former colleagues—who'd been on our first party aboard, soon after the ship had first manifested itself in the Solar System, but who'd elected not to stay—had described it as interactivity on steroids. I could see that, and yet the label failed to properly characterise the ship's nature. It was deeply organic; it wasn't a process.

There was much else we could not discern. None aboard (that we knew of) knew the ship's age, or its origins, or its operators. None aboard (that we knew of) knew how many species of people populated the ship. None aboard (that we knew of) knew its name. Though it was apparently not the only such ship, none aboard (that we knew of) could tell how many such ships there were, within the galaxy and perhaps even further afield. None aboard (that we knew of) knew whether other such ships carried species of people different than those found on this ship. Of course, though, such a thing could be inferred, by analogy, since this was the first such ship to carry human people. That we knew of.

The ship was big, major-asteroid big, minor-moon-of-a-Jovian-planet big, multiple-intertwining-public-transport-systems big. Most of it was made inaccessible to us, for reasons of safety or comfort or seniority. A small portion of it, multilevelled, contiguous, dendritic, was designated as human-only; whether it had been lying fallow before our arrival, or whether several other species of people had ceded portions of their own territory aboard the ship in preparation for our arrival, we couldn't know, and none could tell us. Extending beyond the human-only zone, along several vectors, were shared-access zones, where we could encounter representatives of those aboard with whom it was safe and allowable and feasible to interact, and who presumably represented only a small proportion of the different species of people aboard. Were there other domains within the ship which yet lay unoccupied, awaiting the vessel's arrival in the next inhabited system and an influx of further intelligent life? We did not know. Certainly some sectors, directly abutting those to which we had full or partial access, housed species we hadn't yet met, couldn't yet meet—those we did meet attested to this, though provided no details on these other species—and we had access to, knowledge of, only a minuscule portion of the ship's overall structure. Would this change, given time? There were indications, or perhaps merely expectations, that access to additional species would be earned or conferred with the completion of a probationary period, or perhaps of several sequential probationary periods. Whether these were timed, or tested in some other manner, we didn't know, and none would tell us. Nor were we told whether there was a prospect of failure on our part, nor what circumstances might devolve from that.

Did the ship travel? Clearly it must; it had not been within our solar system before it was, and then it left. But there was no sense of motion, no direction taken, no velocity apparent, no acceleration along a vector. The more technically minded among us—of whom I was not one, and am not one—suggested that the ship, between manifestations in one occupied star system after another, might well exist in some arbitrary location within subspace: nowhere, in effect. Perhaps, our more technically minded argued, the ship did not truly travel, it just appeared, whenever and wherever it chose to.

Where might it appear next? We'd no idea, we weren't told. Possibly it had already visited several star systems after our own, those few months ago now, but if any passengers had been taken on or had disembarked at any of these notional systems, there was no information we could glean. We'd be informed, we supposed, when next we stopped or materialised or instantiated in a star system from where a group of passengers would be moving into one of the domains which fringed ours; but who knew when that might be? Not us.

There was much we could not know.

What did we know? We knew there was no hope of war. Disputes were settled not through combat, but by negotiation and diplomacy, whatever the rules of that diplomacy might be. Our first tour aboard, therefore, was to be purely an intelligence-gathering exercise, accompanied by a noncommittal cultural outreach mission. Observe; learn; avoid errors. Comprehension must precede action.

This we would have stuck to, but the bronters wanted to trade, or at least to negotiate; my superiors didn't wish to cause offence through refusal to enter discussion.

And in just this manner, we had ourselves a situation.

My apologies, I say. I shouldn't stare.

I don't understand this, the bronter responds. *Surely one of your species' primary means of gathering information is the visual. Information is a prized asset. Why should you express regret at gaining it?*

It's a question of propriety, I reply. I already know this to be a meaningless rejoinder: their kind does not have an equivalent concept. They are difficult creatures to offend.

I'm staring, because this bronter has forelimbs; they are a different individual. It is perhaps five days since my earlier encounter, I'm nursing a drink again in the same multispecies rec room—Caal won't bother me here, he never frequents the multispecies facilities—and this is a different bronter. Their translation device is different also: smaller and (I think) newer, without the delay exhibited on the previous instance. Do the others of your kind frequent this space also? I ask them.

I wouldn't know. I have no contact with the other four.

I'm about to correct their numeracy, but something checks me. That must complicate negotiations for you, I say instead. To not directly confer with the others of your kind. I mean, I think I understand why it is so, that's to say the other of your number with whom I spoke previously explained that yours is not in any sense a social species, but surely the negotiation must be a joint outcome for you. I find it difficult to fathom how you negotiate severally to achieve a unified result.

It's who we are, it's how we are, they explain. *When we meet another of our kind, it's an opportunity for reproduction, but also for combat. It is the same for you, I gather.*

Not really. Perhaps on a conceptual level. We're competitive, but cooperative also.

A pause, while the bronter leans forward again, to tongue their drink; they close first two eyes and then the other one. *And have you fathered children yourself, if that's the expression I want?*

It wouldn't be 'fathered' in my case, I say. And no.

My condolences.

It's not a lack in my life, I tell them. Such things are nowadays a choice.

This is strange for me. To produce offspring, it is a wonderful achievement, worthy of the loss of limbs. This compels us, as it must. How can you 'choose' otherwise? Is it that you don't like fucking?

I like fucking just fine, I say, sensing a bloom of colour on my cheeks. But it's possible for us to fu— to interact with another in that way with negligible chance of reproduction.

A longer pause before the bronter's next half-rumbled response, as though unfamiliar thoughts percolate through some subdermal obstacle. *When I consume a rival's arm, I know I'll gestate, will in some months' time regurgitate young. It's a strongly satisfying sensation, a fulfilment of a bodily craving. That's how it is for us. To do that, or to do what I understand is equivalent for your phylum—this conjoining, this fucking—and yet to consciously avoid procreation the while, it must... be odd. All that irksome friction, to no result. The action must be incomplete, disappointing; half-hearted, as you might say.*

One gets used to it, I say, the blush heightening its heat. I sip the drink, ignoring as best I'm able the spearmint aftertaste which now somehow accompanies it, either innately or through the bronter's heat-haze proximity in this otherwise vacant multispecies rec room. But I'd prefer not to get too involved in a discussion of sexual politics.

Sexual politics, they repeat. *Two concepts alien to us.*

I choose to pursue the less personally volatile option, and ask: How can you have a civilisation, and not politics?

It's not necessary. And the idea of your politics, of requiring so many together in one place, it causes me discomfort, or perhaps what you would term shame. This is something we forbid ourselves, as we must; it's something deeply wrong. There would be so much reproduction, then so much eating of young those months later. None of us could protect our young against that onslaught of predation. Many of us would ourselves die, as individuals fought each other for territory. It would be a waste, it would be dangerous for us, it would be devastating. We don't do that. The notion that you do… but then there are so many of you; far, far more than of us. You must all be—what is that term you use? Crowded? Packed together?

We are, I suppose. But thirteen billion across an entire planet… it's still possible to find solitude, perhaps not solitude as you would know it, but still. It's there if you search for it. I enjoy solitude.

That is good to know. Solitude is a lifegoal for us.

Is it difficult for you here? Not conversing with me, I mean, in a more general sense. Aboard the ship. So many different kinds, in a comparatively small space. It must seem confining.

So many, yes, that's so. But not of us. Here there are only five of us, I'm informed, and we never meet. Your kind, the others' kinds, they don't provoke us as we do, each other. Forgive me for saying so, but we see you as animals, not rivals. That's not a judgement, it's an innate reaction for us. Of course we know you are thinking beings, you would not otherwise be here, but it simplifies things for us to see you as animals. I mean no offence.

None taken. I would say that's a common instinctive reaction among sapients of widely different morphologies. It's probably similar for many of us. But how is it you don't meet? Are you rostered?

We are zoned. The ship is big, after all; it's modularised by environment, as you already would know, so as to cater to the requirements and susceptibilities of the different animals aboard. Species aboard, no offence. But beyond that, for a species which is naturally territorial—and our kind is not the only such—the space allotted to that species is further subdivided. It is not what we would have chosen, but it is functional. And we refrain from scent-marking, to avoid provocation. It's... awkward, but the awkwardness is necessary. They close two eyes, then the other. *The dialogue is necessary. The goal is important.*

We probably should not discuss the goal outside a formal setting, I say.

For us, there is no formal, they reply. *Formal goes with social; we don't have such things.*

A different multispecies rec room, dark and somewhat humid, fragranced like rotting hibiscus, inconveniently low-ceilinged.

A bronter would never fit within this space; I scarcely do, myself. Hunch my way to the self-serve area, make a safe selection from the booth's haptograms, collect my drink, navigate to the table at which—on a gritty tray of something which looks like, but doesn't smell like, salt—the small and somewhat shrew-like creature that I seek is lounging. Mouthless, olive green, scaled, long-tailed. I bow—which is to say, I extend the ceiling-enforced stoop further— and take the available chair. It's inconveniently low-seated, but at least I can straighten my back. I turn my attention to the rhatt. It rolls a little on the tray's bed of crystalline grains; the species absorbs nutrients through its skin, so presumably this one is eating, or drinking, or perhaps this is how it gets high. After several seconds, it pauses its motion atop the saltlike substance, turns its diminutive snout towards me. I have an audience.

Have I spoken to you before? I ask.

A chittering hiss precedes by several seconds its translator's vocalisations: the noise of the rhatt itself is cricket-like, though its legs aren't involved in generating the sound. *I cannot be sure.*

Your kind have so few distinguishing features, yes, and you change your disguises daily. That increases the difficulty for us.

Our disguises?

Your—what do you call them? Your raiment? Your garb? Your outfits?

Our clothes.

That word too, yes. And such strange rules you have for those: the crotch must be covered, those glands on your front, but other features not. This would not work for us, no, we require our dermal surface for sustenance. But why should it matter, yes, whether we two have spoken before? It doesn't offend me if we have not. Or is this just a—how do you say it? A pick-up line? A means of beginning a conversation?

Those words mean something different for us, I reply. But I asked because I spoke to one of your kind when I had first come aboard, and he told me—

She. This offends me, yes, that you say you have spoken with one of us before, and do not know that we are always 'she'.

My apologies, I say, striving to inject as much sincerity as possible… a likely pointless endeavour, for if I do not know the gender of this species, then I will certainly not be sufficiently across whatever counts, for them, as body language. I most definitely did not wish to miscategorise your colleague—

I accept your contrition, yes, but please be more careful. The rhatt moves towards the centre of the tabletop, closer to me, which I take to indicate a gesture of trust.

Your colleague, she told me something when I met her. Something she'd gleaned from studying the ship's records, and I was wanting to check—

That would be—[a burst of white noise from the rhatt's translator, a device bigger than herself]. *She is dead now, yes, and she was the only one of us who did that.*

I'm sorry to hear that.

You should not feel sorrow. She lived a long life, yes, and she was widely appreciated. Do you wish to speak to her?

I would have done, yes. But now—

I will set it up for you, then.

But she is dead.

Are you prejudiced?

No, I— I am confused. I suppose I did not consider that it would be possible. With us it would not be.

With us, death ends the activity, yes, but the consciousness is preserved, in a state of dormancy from which it can be reawakened. It must make it difficult for you that this isn't so among your kind.

I don't know how effective this little shrew-like creature's lie-detection abilities are, so I say nothing.

There was Caal, there was a bronter. I was there too, of course. It was horrid, but more through a vague and inescapable sense of menace than through any specific action or definite threat. I woke, unnerved, sweaty, thankfully alone. Already the dream's particulars had let slip their mooring, were adrift, were receding. The sense of menace hung around, like an extra who doesn't realise it's time to quit the stage.

Was it really the case that one bronter had told me there were four aboard, and that another had told me five? I may well have misremembered one or other exchange, and even if I had not there might be any of several innocuous explanations. Perhaps a bronter did not count themself when enumerating; the separate utterances may well have both been versions of *there are four of us, aside from myself of course* which might have been translated differently, though innocently, by their separate translation devices. Or perhaps they were of different castes, operating with different information, or had been allotted a larger or a smaller specific territory on the basis of status— But they hadn't been allotted a specific territory. Their territories plainly overlapped, in a situation where at least one of them had told me they did not. They'd lied, at least one of them had lied to me.

Or had been misinformed.

Or had been mistranslated.

Or I'd misremembered, but I didn't believe that was so.

On the next off-shift, I'm given directions to an unfamiliar location. I ask whether I'll require an environment suit. Apparently not; the venue is still within the multispecies zone, with conditions acceptable to both the human and rhatt metabolisms. A meeting place, I gather; not one we've required, since we are not in formal negotiations with the rhatts.

I'm not sure what to expect of what's effectively a rhatt seance: solemnity, funereality, or perhaps something functionally equivalent to the tackiness of Ouija boards and crystal balls. It's none of that. Just another low-ceilinged room, characteristically dark and muggy, but seemingly empty until I notice the rhatt contingent, encamped upon the broad tabletop: three individuals, a translator, and a scored and somewhat aerodynamic-looking translucent amber lozenge. I've no idea which is the rhatt I spoke with the previous evening, nor who are the other two: relatives of the deceased? Representatives of some rhatt religion? Technicians? Officials?

If it matters, I presume I'll be told.

At least my chair this time is appropriately human-proportioned.

How do we do this? I ask.

You speak, yes, and [burst of static] *will answer,* says the middle rhatt. (Or rather, this is the rhatt from whom the sounds emanate which are converted into comprehensible speech by the translator.)

There's no ceremony, no rites to adhere to?

Why would there be any such thing? You just wish to ask some questions, yes, so you ask her.

What is death like? This I don't ask, partly from a sense of propriety, partly because there's no point. The dead rhatt—whom I have dubbed Rhatt₁ because [burst of static] does not usefully distinguish her from the other rhatt with whom I've spoken—has no knowledge of death, other than the fact that she is dead and can no longer experience the world around her. It's not clear to me whether her current knowledge allows her to comment on things she knew but never discussed in life; the other rhatt I spoke with, Rhatt2, has briefed me only by informing me that *everything can be asked, yes, but not all can be answered.*

You told me earlier, I say now, about one of the races which is no longer represented aboard the ship. Can you reiterate, please? There are some details I've forgotten.

There's an answering hiss from the amber lozenge, sustained and structured; but, though I wait for the translation, it doesn't emerge. When the delay has grown awkward, I turn to Rhatt2 and inform her that I haven't heard the reply.

My apologies. It appears this communication module is not configured for speech from the dead. Please wait, yes, and we will rectify this. Now the two flanking rhatts scamper—there's no other word so apt, though 'scurry' comes close—to the translator, then to the lozenge, then to the translator again, pressing themselves against each device in turn in a manner reminiscent of a cat scent-marking its owner's furniture.

Technicians, I decide, as they move once more to the lozenge. The process takes no more than two minutes; then the tech-rhatts resume their stations either side of Rhatt2.

The lozenge hisses again, and this time the translator relays the semantic content for me. It's largely as I remember it.

What can you tell me of the other former passenger races? I ask.

A portion, yes, but I do not know all. A rhatt's life is only so long, and the ship's information is intended to be species-specific, and is not readily accessed by others. It took me long domains of my time to learn how to read what others had encoded; in all our time aboard this ship, I am only the third rhatt to have studied this technique. Still, the telling would be long, yes, and I do not wish to fatigue you. Perhaps you can describe for me the type of information you're seeking about these now-extinct races?

I'm curious as to the particulars of their species' extinguishment, I say. Especially whether there are any common features.

The lozenge's response takes more than a half hour; I have several further questions, but none I feel I can ask. I thank the lozenge, then the living rhatts in turn, and catch my head painfully on the low ceiling as I stand up.

There are few firm rules aboard the ship, and no visible central authority. One rule, though, is that gossip is not permissible. By 'gossip' I mean that no passenger species is allowed to discuss a second onboard species with a third such species. If you wish to know about a given species, it's necessary to deal with them directly: through dialogue and negotiation and/or by subscription to their cultural presentations. Thus we cannot ask the rhatts what they know of the bronters; they won't tell us. We can only know of the bronters what they tell us of themselves (which plainly will be a subjective view) and what we intuit from our dealings with them (which will also necessarily be subjective).

Oh, and the bronters have no tendency to communicate with each other; therefore, they do not do cultural presentations. Which means, with them, we are operating in an information-poor environment.

The rhatts cannot discuss with us other extant passenger species, but they can discuss with us those species which have, for one reason or another, perished. There is no way of learning whether any of the now-extinct species, as described to me earlier this evening by my little dead friend, had had dealings with the bronters, but my instincts tell me that the big trinocular aliens have been active in negotiations before this. They initiated contact with us so soon, and their official lines of communication have been consistent from the outset. (And how does a race so hermitic, so territorial-on-steroids even manage such a feat?

They must in some manner converse with each other, despite their assurances otherwise.)

Rhattı described for me about a dozen now seemingly fully extinct species; she stated that there were numerous others on which she did not have useful detail. We know, or believe we know, that there are several dozen, perhaps upwards of a hundred, still-living passenger species aboard the ship, so there's no solid reason to suspect the involvement of the bronters in the demise of any of the races described for me by the consciousness, or the ghost, or the memory, of Rhattı. And yet three of those races perished some centuries, or some millennia, or some rhatt-specific multigenerational time interval after negotiating—with some unknown species in each instance—the transfer, to that other species, of territorial rights to an uninhabited planetary body within their home star system. Just like the bronters, and their expressed intent to acquire Mars from us.

I do not trust the bronters, but I have nothing solid on which to base that mistrust. Just gossip, from the dead about the dead.

My apologies, I say. It's impolite of me to stare.

The bronter, this room-dominating slab of muscle and maw and scar tissue, shows no familiarity towards my once-more-repeated opening gambit; can they genuinely be a different individual than either of the two I've previously encountered? Or are they feigning a lack of recollection? Or do they simply not recognise me, one of the—to-them—numerous indistinct human animals aboard the ship? Or is it that I, ignorant of their body language, just do not know how to perceive recognition in a bronter? They briefly close two eyes. *I don't consider it impolite, they reply,* the translator's tone mellifluous and somehow schoolmarmish. *Thus you need not.*

I have to ask, will your other forelimb grow back?

I am hopeful. The process takes longer each time.

This is how you reproduce, yes? Forgive my impertinence; this is a strange reproductive mechanism, from my kind's perspective.

It's strange you find it so. For us, of course, it is the most natural thing.

And you fight if you encounter one another, is that correct? To the death?

Often, yes. It must be so, of course, to avert overpopulation. Unless both parties lose limbs in the encounter. Then the combat stops short of death, out of respect for the new lives which result.

It must be difficult for you in some respects, here on the ship. How is it that the three of you avoid this combat?

They lean forward, far enough that the canister of drink is enveloped in the maw, there's a fluid noise, a plumbing noise almost, and when they lean back the canister is empty. They briefly close two eyes. *We never meet.*

And how is that arranged, or enforced? Is there a schedule?

Yes. And now that I think on it, there are more of us than three. Five or six of us, I think. Though of course we never meet.

Who sets the schedule? If it is not impolite of me to ask this.

It's inappropriate of you to ask; I will not answer.

My apologies.

No need. You are not to blame for your species' ignorance, you have not been here long. In time, you'll learn all this.

You bronters have been here a long time, I gather. I mean, not necessarily you personally, but your kind. Is there also a schedule for your attendance on this vessel? Again, my apologies in advance if this is an impertinent question.

The question's acceptable. There's no schedule. We serve our lives here.

That's interesting. You must have seen many species in your time aboard. Of course I can't discuss particulars with you, of other races aboard, but not all of them remain, do they?

Your meaning is unclear.

I mean that some races board, partake in a series of negotiations, and leave the vessel. And some of those races that leave the vessel become extinct.

We would know nothing of this. This conversation approaches impropriety.

Once more, my apologies. And yet I find the subject fascinating. I'll say no more on it; I've no wish to cause offence, after all.

Again, you're not to blame for your ignorance.

Thank you. Can I ask, is it difficult for you to be here? To have left your world, and to never see your offspring again?

I will go now, says the bronter. There's a touch of the tectonic in the way they rise from their seat.

They leave behind the brushed-metal canister from which they had been drinking. On a whim, I purloin it.

I should have seen it before. If the bronters never meet, but if their communications with regard to the ongoing negotiation are consistent, then it follows they are also in negotiation with at least one other race, from which process they are indirectly able to communicate with other bronters. This I've understood for a while.

But what I see now is: there's an alternative explanation, perhaps a simpler one. Again, I've no proof. Nor can I feasibly secure any. I'm sure of it now, though, nonetheless.

I ponder a tussle between bronters. One loses their forelimbs; now the other will bear young. The wounds must be a disadvantage, may well be hideously painful, but those creatures cannot be easy to kill; the task requires commitment. My mind tells me it's a brutal act, barbaric, merciless.

On the other hand, are the activities of we humans any better?

*

Stay, Gerda says softly to me, while the others file out of the briefing room. I resume my seat, idly watch Caal's back as he departs.

Is there something I can assist with? I ask.

The pause is long enough for discomfort, and when it's broken, this is done with just one word: Birgit.

I wait, several seconds again, while she busies herself with polishing her spectacles on the hem of her blouse. Is there—

Birgit, we're all of us a team.

Yes, I reply. (She has learnt of me and Caal. But if that's the case, why is he not also—)

There aren't so many of us here, this place is strange and unpredictable. She waves her hand at the briefing room's wall fixtures, the clichéd auto-responsive repros of the Grand Canyon, the Amazon, Kilimanjaro, Svalbard, then adds: It's important we remain a team. Gerda is emphasising each word, as though they have been cast in precious metal. Or have been presented to her from above.

By Caal. It has to be. But I've no notion why. Aloud: I agree, of course. Have I given any cause to seem otherwise? Because—

The folds at the side of her mouth are tight; she's not comfortable with this conversation. Which strengthens my conviction that it's not her choice to be doing this. She says now: This is a difficult task, a vital task we're doing here. We need all to be able to trust each other implicitly. The social program recognises this.

The social program. It's hard not to snicker, to keep my mouth serious. I ask: Are you saying I should be participating in the karaoke?

Not necessarily that, but *something*, Birgit. We have improv, we have cards evenings, we have roleplaying campaigns in various genres; there's billiards and table tennis. Chess tournaments. Library time, where you can read in the company of others, if reading is your preference. You're not at any of it, Birgit. Once the work is done, you're just gone. And why is that?

I take my time before I answer. I'm not really a social person, I say. I'm fairly sure I said as much on my application. Is there any evidence that my teamwork is lacking? In the meetings, in the assignments I take on?

No, says Gerda, and shrugs. The light, this diffuse light which emanates from nowhere particular within the room, manages somehow to catch on her glasses. The work is good, that's why you were taken on, she says. But we need to see more of you.

Why?

Because if things go bad, we all need to know we can trust one another. That won't happen if you make yourself the outsider.

Caal's told me things won't go bad; but I don't say this, of course. I can't tell Gerda, my direct supervisor, that I am fucking hers. Or rather, that I had been, because it's done now, and past. You can trust me, I say. Everyone on the team can trust me. I recognise the opportunity this gives us, as a society, and I want us to do the best with that.

So where do you go?

I consider simply saying that I remain in my quarters, but likely Gerda knows this isn't the case. I visit the multispecies districts, I say.

Why?

The question throws me a little, in its simplicity and naïveté. Gerda, I say, we're on a starship. This is something so far beyond our species' current technological capability, it's an unparallelled opportunity for us, for all of us. No offence, but I don't feel like wasting that opportunity, when it's offered to me, by enduring a snooker evening, or a series of table tennis grudge matches. I'm going to see the sights, to the extent possible. And since we're not able to view subspace as we travel through it, or to gain any of the secrets of the ship's function or structure, I'm going to do the next best thing: I'm going to meet the creatures.

You put it like that, says Gerda, and something about her newly cleaned spectacles displeases her: she removes them, checks them, puts them on again. Adds: But you're missed, at these social events. People start talking. People start wondering. And now you say you've been meeting other species, on the quiet. You're not in the cultural contingent, Birgit, you're in Diplomatic Support. People in Diplomatic Support should not be meeting with the aliens in their spare time. It has the potential to jeopardise everything we're working for here.

How? I ask. I'm not present in any of the negotiations, so what can I tell them which would threaten that? Nothing that isn't already public knowledge, that they could and probably have heard already from the cultural reps. (Except that's not true, I realise. I know things I shouldn't, because of Caal. But I strongly sense that my continuance in this role is dependent on keeping that aspect locked away.)

So why meet with them?

Jesus on a goat, Gerda, because I'd be *bored* otherwise. I don't want to waste my time here with shuffleboard and pin-the-tail-on-the-donkey and whatnot. I meet them because I'm interested in what's happening here, and because I think a part of my role as an advisor is to ensure that the advice I provide is informed, for fuck's sake. My apologies, I didn't mean to raise my voice like that.

It's fine. We have to be able to express ourselves, after all. But I want you to limit your contact with them. You're one of us, Birgit, you should be spending more time among us than among them.

(I *do* spend more time among 'us'.) Understood. Shuffleboard and charades, then.

Birgit.

She could have asked: Who have you met?

She could have asked: What is it you discuss with them? What have you learnt? What have you let slip? It's staggering that she didn't.

It's a clear indication that, even if he was the driving force for that little intervention, she doesn't know anything about the thing with Caal. So now I suppose the vital thing is to ensure it stays that way.

Actually, no. The vital thing is to ensure that we don't get shafted by the bronters.

We'll give them Mars, we'll never get Mars back. And we'll gain nothing in return.

We must not give them Mars.

It's me, I announce at the door to Nanya's quarters. Birgit.

The door slides open. If Nanya's surprised to see me, it doesn't show. Tea? she asks, as she invites me in. Hangings, cushions, a garishly draped bed, a functional table-and-two-chairs arrangement in one corner. A fragrance, jasmine I think, though I'm never sure of such things; flamenco guitar, barely audible. I feel ashamed, almost, at my own quarters' sparse fitout.

I'm not one for fuss, but sometimes fuss is attractive.

Real tea? I ask.

Near enough.

Water will do fine. Thank you.

I heard you were kept back by Gerda this afternoon. Anything up? Or shouldn't I ask?

No, it's fine. Apparently I need to up my backgammon, or my paintball minigolf, or some such.

I just can't with that nonsense, Nanya replies, smiling, then adds, as she hands me a tumbler of iced water: But it's not like you to make social calls.

Yes, no, I have a question. How would someone go about measuring the apparent gravity field in the human-habitation zone aboard the ship?

Oh, I can tell you that straight off. It's ten point three, about one gee plus five percent.

Slightly stronger than Earth, then?

Yes.

It's that across the entire zone?

As near as I can tell. Is this somehow important for the diplomatic brief?

I was just looking to make sense of something I'd heard.

And this does that?

I think so, yes. Thank you.

Next, the multispecies rec room. Unoccupied on this occasion, and absent any bronter topnote; nonetheless, I still feel self-conscious as I step into, then out of, then into the shared space once more, feeling my balance as I do so.

The quality of the air changes slightly, and the temperature, and the light and acoustics. But if there's a transition, a shift in my perceived weight that accompanies these, it's too small for me to sense.

They were lying about this too.

Nestled, I say: Include me in the negotiating team. The face-to-face, not just the backroom stuff.

You know I can't do that, says Caal, his stubble against my cheek, his arm warm around my midriff. It would mean my role, if it came out I'd pulled strings.

But you *can* pull strings, I say. You know I can make a positive difference to the negotiations. I've gained useful background knowledge.

Such as?

The family history of each of the bronters here. It can give us an insight into their motivations. I can help sharpen whatever bargain we strike with them. You can't tell me that wouldn't be useful.

Workshop it for me, says Caal.

I press back against him, feeling his response, and slowly start to speak.

Seven of us; one bronter.

It's taken time, it's taken measures I'd have preferred to avoid, but I'm here now. I wait while the others have their say, then I signal an intent to comment. Caal believes he knows what's coming next, the platitudes I've practised with him.

Your offspring are precious to you, I say. That's so, isn't it?

It's so, says the bronter. They briefly close one eye while the other two remain fixed on me.

It must be difficult, I say. To have spent most of your lifespan on this ship, and to know you will not see your offspring ever again. And worse than that—at least for us it would be worse—to know that every other of your kind whom you might encounter, here on this ship, is a mortal foe. I imagine we all of us around our side of this table can sympathise with that difficulty in your circumstances. I pause, look to my right and then to my left, seeking inclusion before I return my attention to the bronter. I nod, they close one eye.

I've something here to show you, I say, and reach into my satchel. I quickly extract from a sealed pouch an object which I place on the tabletop and then push as close as possible to the bronter. There's a movement of their arms, quickly arrested: not towards the object, but towards my own extended forearm.

I lean back, my pulse racing—those creatures are faster than I thought—and raise my voice: But it's not the truth, is it? You're all of you—

That's all I can get out, or possibly less than that. Gerda mutes the team's translator, glowers at me; Caal looks aghast—furious—but I don't care. I've said what I came to say, done what I came to do, and will face whatever consequences devolve from this. There's a noise, not a pleasant one, from the slab-faced alien.

These negotiations are terminated, their translator informs us, while the bronter stares at—but doesn't otherwise react to—the scent-marked canister that remains within their arms' reach. Then, grabbing their translator, they rise thunderously from their seat.

The ship is an alien place, which we knew it would be, from the start; something synonymous with strangeness. Wars are not fought between these species, or so we've been told; dialogue is the weaponry wielded here, and I've drawn blood.

It wasn't a difficult lie to see through; indeed, it's almost laughable that they expected us not to see it. Perhaps their minds work differently, perhaps it's a fiction they've employed successfully in the past, those bronters, with their own species or others, and perhaps it therefore seemed robust to them.

The bronters on the ship were an undisclosed family group, a parent (or maybe two) and several siblings; they could coexist without combat because of relatedness. They were therefore not genuinely representative of their kind; it's likely any deal they brokered would not be recognised as valid by the broader bronter population. We'd never have gained a world in exchange for Mars. I reported as much to Gerda, in my dismissal interview.

I'm off the diplomatic team, of course, even in a support function. Gerda has told me I can shred all hope of a career. But they can't imprison me, there's none of that here, so I've been relegated to Cultural.

(Caal, allegedly: Cultural? That's a fucking joke! She's not a creator, she's a destroyer!)

Is it possible I was mistaken about the bronters? Of course. I don't believe I was, they were plainly lying to us, but it's possible nevertheless that I've jinxed the best deal humanity was ever going to get here. It's possible I've been played by the rhatts, or by some unseen agency. I don't care. It still feels right, what I did. There'll be other negotiations, which they'll have to manage without me.

I still explore the shared spaces. Not the bronter corridor, of course; but there's still the rhatts, and several others. Some of the peoples are fascinating, and Cultural gives me more leeway to learn about them. But tonight I'm not in the frame of mind for such exploits, I need a break from all that.

I'll do as Gerda would want, for once. I'll go try my hand on the croquet lawn.

NEGATIVE REVIEW

This is a story about the first manned landing on Mercury.

It's not the first story about a manned landing on Mercury.

This story contains: Men. Rockets. Spacesuits. The planet Mercury. A mysterious alien presence. Aspirations toward a sense of wonder.

This story does not contain: Women. Nuanced commentary on today's society. A realistic method of propulsion. A sense of wonder.

This story solves problems with jargon.

This story creates problems with jargon.

In this story, a horrific sacrifice is required of the protagonist. And of the reader.

In this story, the main characters end well. That's something, I suppose.

BETTER THAN ONE

Thanks to the 2040 raw milk amnesia pandemic, many people have already forgotten what it was like to live through that mercifully brief stretch in the mid-2030s when the Extra Head movement was at its zenith.

It had started, as do so many retrospectively ill-judged fads, with the billionaire class: active-volcano lair construction had become passé, gold-plated private jets had lost their shine, the surreptitious drone-bombing of each other's superyachts with orca sex pheromones was no longer the thrill ride it had been, so what more logical next step could there have been, in the ever-present techbroligarch arms race to seize notoriety, attention and adulation? The double-headed megarich began to crop up like so many twin-cap mushrooms.

As transplant costs fell, televangelists, upwardly mobile pentesters, YouTube influencers spruiking their grandmothers' secret recipes for biblically accurate angel food cakes, well-heeled hair-metal guitarists and try-hard Zaphod Beeblebrox impersonators all got in on the act.

Some even took it further. The acclaimed Mixed Martial Archery contestant and incelebrity Andrew Moma-Guggenheim famously had himself equipped with three heads, each with a field of view 120 degrees apart from the other two. Moma-Guggenheim declared that, with this wraparound vision, he was [sic] 'imperious to ambush attacks'.

He went on to win two full seasons of the controversial but popular livestreamed deathmatch sport before being tragically killed by a falling piano.

Other proponents of bicapitalism met less exquisitely choreographed ends, often as a consequence of transplant rejection, a phenomenon which became so frequent that it led to the collapse of the trillion-dollar body augmentation startup NogginGraft following the shock revelation that their popular line of 'vat-grown' heads were not in fact vat grown but were, rather, harvested in a manner which really should have surprised no-one except, perhaps, the obscenely wealthy and, perhaps briefly, their unwitting donors. Cashed-up transplant recipients sought desperate remedies, documented most memorably, for those who'd steered clear of the raw milk, in headlines such as 'Heads Roll As Clinic Guillotinist Loses Count' and 'Severance Payout: Board Seeks Hefty Capital Outlay After Wrong Head Removed'. The federal government begrudgingly passed a law or two, removing attractive tax concessions for the double-header class but stopping short of the introduction of the hefty Extra Neck Tax which some economists had called for.

With regulation and the threat of more of same on the way, the movement dwindled. Almost overnight the surviving members of the uberinfluentsia turned their backs on the fad, investing their funds in less outrageous pursuits such as the cloning of antimatter whippets and the construction of increasingly large Greek god mechas as a means of personal transport.

Nowadays the only reminders of the Extra Head epoch—aside, of course, from largely unread nostalgia-porn columns such as this one—are the once-wealthy beggars whose chunky hand-knitted turtlenecks may hide their decapitation scars but not their abiding shame at such a disfiguring loss of status and face.

SLOWBOAT

*Let ψ denote the conceptspace of stories set upon an interstellar slowboat, with **i** the number of cryopreserved passengers awoken by the inciting incident and **j** the number of passengers who remain viable or revivable at the story's end. In this story, located solidly within ψ-space, the product **ij** equals zero. Start.*

The ship was big; the ship was old. When it was new it had functioned flawlessly, and it had continued to function on the cusp of flawlessness for several centuries, but the ship was much older than that now. It had been designed to be self-repairing, and for the mechanisms which rectified those self-repairing features to be self-maintaining, and for the apparatuses which restored to functionality those self-maintaining mechanisms when they failed (as they sometimes would) to be also self-restoring. For a long time, a very long time as humans would measure it, this concatenation of connective and corrective mechanisms all worked very well, a stochastic clockwork; but ten thousand, twenty thousand, thirty thousand years is a span of time far beyond the comprehension of any systems architect, for all they might have argued otherwise. The ancient ship, still on its maiden voyage across night's ocean, now showed its age in a myriad mostly minor ways: in irregularities in the decking across which the mobile autonomous repair/maintenance unit Marmu-437P rolled; in imperfections in the controls of the multiple airlocks which separated sector from sector, and which Marmu-437P would open and then close behind it in sequence as it trundled its solitary way through the ship's cryospaces twice every daycycle; in small but disturbing thermal fluctuations between or across sectors, where the ship had been designed to maintain a consistency of temperature as good as stasis; in scuffing and wear, an increasing fraction of which was directly attributable to the patient ministrations of the little mobile unit; in the gradual patch-by-patch failure of status panels; in brief bursts of sound which, as often as not now, remained unexplained, their origins unsourced. Were Marmu-437P capable of such a human sensation as annoyance, these and many other aspects of the ship's ages-long degradation would have so qualified; but the unit knew patience, and quiet calm, and so was simply disconcerted by these things, some of which represented tasks which it would need to address, others of which were aspects of gradual decline about which it could do nothing. The ship would not last forever; nothing mechanical could endure indefinitely; it was by no means certain that the ship would endure to reach its destination, with Marmu-437P its last agent of repair, its sole bulwark against terminal dysfunction.

And Marmu-437P was, by design and construction, no generalist, where it was imperative in the present circumstance that it should be. The unit's original purpose had been as a propulsion-systems troubleshooting device, a role sparsely required on a thirty-five-millennia-long voyage during which the propulsion systems need only be kept online for the first decade or so following launch, while the ship was under acceleration to achieve its intended cruising velocity, and then brought online again for the voyage's projected final decade or so, when the ship would be required to decelerate as it neared its destination. The limited demands placed upon the mobile unit by this crucial yet highly specialised inspection and maintenance task accounted for Marmu-437P's longevity while the many other mobile autonomous devices aboard the ship had gradually failed; as, too, had their improvised replacements; as, too, had those systems which had fabricated those replacements; as, too, had those mechanisms which had sought to maintain the ship's critical construction capabilities. In sum, Marmu-437P was a highly ruggedised unit long kept unpowered and only comparatively recently reactivated following the terminal decline of the last of the ship's other autonomous mechanisms. This, then, was the sole mobile unit remaining in active service when the trouble started. Or rather, because this is not at all the same thing, this was the sole mobile unit in active service when the long-fomenting trouble was first detected.

Aspects of the backstory have been placed well outside the frame of the story itself. This is intentional and appropriate. Space is big. Time, too, for that matter. Assess.

Marmu-437P didn't understand human hierarchy—human was human, one somewhat squishy, oddly shaped sac of fragile biomolecules was much the same as another—but it was keenly aware, nonetheless, that a human hierarchy existed: this strange perception among humans that one had an intrinsically greater value than another, a value utterly unrelated to (and often in direct opposition to) the number of probable life-years remaining in a human's span. Because of this incomprehension, Marmu-437P's discovery in revival facility 7B—that the frozen forms of several humans had been compromised—was uncoloured by any calculation of the heightened ascribed worth of those particular forms: they were specialists, or they were highly wealthy, or they were very wealthy specialists, or they happened to be the personal favourites or offspring of someone within one of these categories, but they were, foremost, frozen humans just as were the other one-point-two million frozen humans to be found on board the ship, of neither more nor less importance than any others. The detection of a stain—filamentary, reddish-brown—within the ice sheaths separately jacketing five of 7B's cryopassengers was unexpected, and thus concerning, the more because Marmu-437P was unwilling to break the seal on any of the revival casques to obtain a physical sample of the intruding matter. Safeguarding of the human lives in storage was the central responsibility of the ship's mechanisms, but the sole mobile unit which now held this responsibility was ill-designed for such a role, and acutely aware of such ill-design. Identification of the problem would thus depend on Marmu-437P's analytical abilities, and in this area, too, those abilities were sharply limited. It would be fair to say that Marmu-437P did not even properly understand the cryopreservation process, but after all it had never needed to; it was sufficient for the unit to know that, provided the cryochambers' red-line thermal thresholds were not breached, then it was more or less guaranteed that the frozen bodies were maintained in good order. Now it appeared some of them were not in good order, or at least it appeared some of them were encased in ice which, in some measure, was not; and it was Marmu-437P's problem to deal with because there was nothing else here with the capability for the independent action which the circumstance must sooner or later require. For a time after the disturbing discovery, the mobile unit contemplated reviving one or more of the cryopassengers, because it would certainly be possible to identify several with the appropriate cryomedical and physicochemical expertise to address this problem; but to do so would require swapping out one of the revival casques, and this went against Marmu-437P's core programming. Which was a pity, all told, because it meant that the conundrum—of what to do about this possibly indirect hazard facing the obscurely high-value frozen sacs of fragile biochemicals in revival facility 7B—could not be delegated to something else, or indeed, someone else, while the mobile unit busied itself with the distinctly more straightforward and better-suited task of checking and rechecking that the ship's drive systems, when they were ultimately repowered and reignited, would function as required.

It was necessary, Marmu-437P decided, to explore how widespread might be the problem which the stained ice represented. The stain's sighting had been a chance event, and afterwards the mobile unit could not identify what had motivated it to check those casques more carefully than was usually the case: its inspection of the casques was generally a cursory act. There were upwards of a thousand such items onboard, after all, and so long as the thermal trace of each apparatus showed congruence with acceptable tolerances—which, thus far, had always been the case—then the only other potential issue with which Marmu-437P would need to concern itself was to confirm the structural integrity of each casque's casing and instrumentation controls, with which again there had always been an unproblematic compliance. But now there was this new finding, which Marmu-437P had noticed on a whim, as it were, as the unit applied an unusual degree of scrutiny, perhaps having peripherally caught a reflection of light within the ice which had conveyed some illusion of movement. A machine analogue, then, of the phenomenon which humans called the ghost, this idea that something was there which was not in truth there. Yes, perhaps that was how it had happened, the detection; and then, curiosity inflamed, the inspection of the next several casques, four more of which showed the same disquieting feature. The stained ice. Which was in truth there, which was not an illusion, which was not a ghost. It was concerning, it was incipiently unsettling, and it would need to be addressed and, if possible, remedied. By the mobile unit, because nothing else was here. Except the stain.

*

*Let **v** represent the stylespace of stories featuring a nonliving protagonist; let **σ** signify the voicespace of stories characterised by unreliable narration. In this story, a location within **v**-space is already clear, a relationship to **σ**-space less so. Prepare.*

Chamber 3A. A broad corridor-like hall, its floor and ceiling subtly curved to match the contours of the slowly turning hull; an expanse lined with rows of sturdy shelving on which were stowed a multitude of rectangular prisms of ice in one of several standardised sizes, foil-skinned for insulation, containment, and safety, each prism containing a frozen human dreamlessly passing between the stars. Eighty thousand or more such prisms in this one chamber, which extended almost to the vanishing point that marked the ship's prow. Here, as in facility 7B, there had been nothing thermally untoward across the entire recorded extent of the ship's voyage. By this measure, therefore, there should not be a problem here, but the same could have been said of 7B, as had now been proven false. The foil wrapper on each ice-encased human precluded straightforward inspection of the contained ice, but Marmu-437P had travelled here prepared: it had brought with it a coring device, scrupulously cleaned and sterilised; twenty pristine sample tubes in which to collect ice samples; and twenty cleanroom-standard adhesive seals to repair the foil skin's sampling aperture. The mobile unit approached the ninth berth on the shelf to its left and took and labelled a sample, then trundled ahead a short distance, as single-minded as an old-school Mars rover methodically exploring an ancient crater, to obtain its next sample from a berth on the facing shelf.

Of twenty harvested ice samples, selected arbitrarily from the ice-encased bodies in 3A, eighteen showed definite staining broadly consistent with the earlier detections in Facility 7B. There was a substantial physical separation between 3A and 7B, and

Marmu-437P's sampling sites within Chamber 3A had also been broadly spaced to ensure a representatively randomised set of results. The clear implication was that the observed contamination was widespread amidst the cryopassengers. There was no mechanism Marmu-437P could understand which would allow the stain, whatever it might be, to spread from one self-contained ice-prism to another, at an arbitrary distance. It must, therefore, have arisen independently in numerous locations; it might, conceivably, affect virtually all of the ship's freighted humans. But how had it developed? Marmu-437P's initial hypothesis was that it was a consequence of cosmic radiation of some form. This could account for its apparent pervasiveness, but it did not satisfy as an explanation: the ship's hull was effectively impervious to all manifestations of cosmic radiation except for the background neutrino flux, and absorption of neutrinos by ice was a sufficiently improbable event that the extent of staining captured by the samples would have required a voyage duration many orders of magnitude beyond the thirty thousand years which Marmu-437P knew to have elapsed since launch.

But if the staining were not radiative in origin, and could not be rationalised as some form of cross-contamination from ice-sheathed body to ice-sheathed body, what other option existed? It must, somehow, be something innate.

All of this Marmu-437P considered as it cautiously swapped out its lubricating fluid for a formulation better suited to long exposure to the heightened chill of the ship's cryostorage sector: a necessary act of self-maintenance, though not without risk. The unit then set about acquiring skills which were not intrinsically its own: skills of analysis, which were gained quickly; and skills of fabrication and manual improvisation, which were not. The skills of analysis required by Marmu-437P were in the domains of biochemistry, molecular biology, cellular structure, genetics, forensic pathology: the complete crystallised expert knowledge in these fields (or at least that fraction of expert knowledge which had already become crystallised thirty-odd millennia ago, prior to the slowboat's launch) was available in the ship's data archives, and needed merely to be incorporated, practised, and integrated; this took a month, and if in that month other knowledge which had previously been in the mobile unit's purview was shed to make room, what of it? The discarded knowledge could always be reaccessed in future, if it became necessary to do so; that was just how memory worked. The skills of manual improvisation which Marmu-437P needed were associated with the repair and modification of cryomedical equipment which had primarily been designed for purposes of cryopassenger revival; this was the equipment that Marmu-437P must adapt to search for the cellular and biomolecular details which it would need to understand how the ice-stain had arisen, and to understand what the stain even was. This process, which necessitated relocation of revival facility 7B's frozen cargo, took substantially longer than the standard lifetime of a warm human, and resulted in the collateral decommissioning of more than half the facility's available revival units. The infliction of such damage in the ship's collective capability went against Marmu-437P's primary programming, or really it would be more accurate to say that this damage set up a heightened conflict of potentials within Marmu-437P, because it was exactly as necessary to inquisite the hazard which the ice-staining might represent for all the ship's deep-frozen humans as it was to safeguard the technology by which those humans would be decanted from their personal matrix of ice on arrival at the ship's destination. For all this time, Marmu-437P laboured against its internalised conflicting potentials (as well as its long-stanging indifference to the details of human physiognomy with which it was now forced to acquaint itself) (as well as the slow stochastic degradation of its own aging components, some of these now irreplaceable) (as well as the disquieting realisation that it was now no more than three failure points away from irrevocable mechanical dysfunction) (as well as the extended exposure to cryonic chill, for which it was ill-designed), and ultimately won out.

To travel from one star system to another is an exercise in perceptual relativity, requiring either the application of highly spacetime-distorting velocity or of cryonic immobilisation of those transported, or sometimes even both. Does the present story's denouement similarly require the second process, or is such detail incidental? Consider.

Of the more than a million humans in storage on the slowboat, slightly more than a thousand had a numerical identifier ending in '437', and of these there were twenty-nine which bore the suffix P. The mobile unit systematically avoided selection of any of these latter twenty-nine cryopassengers during its ever more extensive sampling endeavours. Perhaps this behaviour amounted to ritual, perhaps the unit instead identified more strongly with those sharing its own identifier, and wished not to find evidence of potential harm to these individuals; perhaps it considered sampling of the ice encasing these individuals to correspond in some way to an assault on, or investigation of, its own machine mortality. This characteristic is offered here without full explanation to the reader, in plainly incomplete compensation for the absence of any more intriguing personality traits associated with the story's sole and rather undemonstrative protagonist.

For the narrative's sake it can now be stated simply, though the discovery process was highly protracted and beset by numerous obstacles. The stain was an organism: cellular in structure, microbial in nature. Marmu-437P was with some difficulty able to determine its genome; or rather genomes, for there were minor differences in the precise genetic sequences of stain samples.

This finding, of clear relatedness alongside evidence of modest genetic diversity, was a clue to the stain's origin, which was of course one of the questions Marmu-437P wished to answer, for the microbe was one previously unknown to science. For several years, as its analysis progressed towards the problem's solution, the mobile unit hypothesised that the stain's presence within the cryopassengers' encasing ice was a result of contamination, most likely introduced during or immediately following the chilldown of each human. Opposing this argument was Marmu-437P's awareness that, across the limited number of short-duration cryonic flights to the outermost planets and Kuiper Belt planetoids which had been completed before the slowboat's Solar System departure, no such contamination had been reported. While the absence of contamination on those earlier, much shorter voyages did not in itself disprove contamination's occurrence on Marmu-437P's slowboat, such occurrence as was now observable would have needed to be so widespread as to imply serious biocontainment errors across each of the more than forty different facilities which had been occupied with the preparation of the slowboat's frozen passengers. Such a comprehensive lapse in cryomedical standards appeared vanishingly improbable. Marmu-437P was forced eventually to conclude that widespread contamination had not occurred during the initial cryogenic procedure.

As it continued its elucidation of the genomes of an ever-increasing proportion of the harvested stain samples, the mobile unit next returned to the previously discounted possibility that the mysterious microbial intruder had in some manner insinuated itself within the passengers' ice jackets during the long centuries of frozen flight, from outside or through some mechanism of transference; but again, there was no evidence to support this, nor could any process be identified which would allow such profligate migration across the hermetic foil *cordon sanitaire* enshrouding each passenger's frozen casing.

Marmu-437P was brought finally to an unwelcome conclusion: the stain's source had been the bodies themselves. The humans were leaking, from frozen tissue into ice, in a manner yet undiscovered. It was, in a word, disgusting (or would have appeared so, to an entity capable of such a subjective reaction, which, as we have already seen, the mobile unit was not); but no other explanation sufficed.

Let $\mathbf{f}(\tau_n)$ represent the story's adoption of elements contained within the set of tropes broadly characteristic of the 'hard science fiction' subgenre, a method used here to allow the story to pass as hard sf without the need for quantitative rigor in the defined setting or narrative. Here three elements from the trope-set τ_n have been recognisably deployed: τ_1, the assumption that a genuine machine intelligence is achievable through sustained technological advancement; τ_2, the assumption that faster-than-light travel is not achievable, necessitating that any human-engineered traversal of interstellar distance must occur at velocities substantially below lightspeed; τ_3, the assumption that unproblematic revival of human travellers from a state of cryosuspension can be considered sufficiently feasible as to provide an effective means to settlement of extrasolar planets through slower-than-light interstellar travel. A fourth element, too, is identifiable, which we might therefore call τ_4: the implicit centrality within the story of some conundrum capable of solution or resolution by a process of investigation. Note that while τ_4 is here represented by the mystery of the stained ice, in its overall scope this element, as generally defined, is not solely a feature contained within the purview of the set τ_n, nor is it even necessarily enclosed within the larger set of all tropes exclusive to the broader science fiction genre; it is also found within much crime fiction, as well as journalism, as well as elsewhere.

Does a fifth element also exist? Yes. Yes, it does, and it is pivotal. But this story is not that movie. Continue.

*

Each passenger a deep-frozen sac of fragile biomolecules: feedstock, in other words, for an opportunistic chemotroph seemingly ideally adapted to cryonic conditions: in other words, a psychrophile, a cold-loving organism.

As Marmu-437P's meticulous investigation continued, it was established that the microbe appeared not to be primarily enteric, but rather showed a broader propensity to skein itself into the ice from the humans' heads, from their torsos, from their limbs. The cuticles, in particular, appeared to be a favoured exit point, and to a lesser extent the ears. Marmu-437P learnt, too, the thermal characteristics of the microbe's metabolism: when cultured in ice with an appropriate nutrient, the psychrophile displayed the greatest propensity for growth, as measured by lateral proliferation through the ice on a decade-by-decade basis, in a temperature range between -180 and -110 °C. The baseline temperature for the cryopassengers' storage, -196 °C, was below this preferred range, yet not utterly inhospitable to the organism. This accounted for the observed microbial manifestations, though not their origins. Marmu-437P also learnt that the psychrophile ceased utterly to metabolise at temperatures exceeding approximately -80 °C, passing into a durable spore form, capable of maintaining subsequent viability after refreezing from temperatures as high as +102 °C. The spores were also highly resistant to all the forms of chemical attack to which Marmu-437P was able to subject them. The resilience of these spores provoked in Marmu-437P a cascade of speculation, triggering hazardous potentials within the mobile unit's decision-making structures:

Was it possible that the spores had been brought aboard the ship, unwittingly present (and undetected) among the humans' own internal microbial flora?

Was it possible, therefore, that the spores were a widespread and undetected component of the terrestrial biosphere at the time of the slowboat's launch?

Was it possible, therefore, that the spores had been circulating within the terrestrial biosphere for centuries, or perhaps even for much longer, preceding the slowboat's launch?

Sporulation represented a quiescent state, attained when the active bacterium could no longer flourish. Was it possible, therefore, that the spores had been waiting with near-infinite patience for a return to the thermal characteristics of some earlier heyday during which the microbe had last prospered?

But if this were so, it was not clear what earlier period of Earth's history might have yielded temperatures sufficiently low for the microbe to proliferate. Neither the ice ages of the past few million years nor the far more ancient and long-enduring Snowball Earth phase would have placed the planet's hydrosphere within the microbe's target temperature range.

Was it possible, therefore, that the spore-forming psychrophile was a truly primordial organism, as old as—or even older than— life on Earth itself?

Marmu-437P was ill-designed to address, or even to contain, such questions, but there was nothing else aboard which could consider them.

τ_5, an unanticipated discovery throws possible light on the origin of life. Or: τ_5, the limits of biological adaptability are once again shown to be more diverse than was understood. Or: τ_5, the nutritional value of a human body should not be discounted, just because the human mind prefers, for personal if somewhat selfish reasons, not to dwell on this aspect. Or: τ_5, perseverance wins, but it's a long game. Proceed.

There was, perhaps, nothing special about this voyage beyond its duration. If problems of resurgent psychrophile infestation had not manifested themselves on any of the previously completed cryosleep voyages of which Marmu-437P had any knowledge—which were the several decades-long traversals to various Kuiper Belt destinations—then that apparent absence of any adverse outcome perhaps did not indicate a specific failure of hygiene upon this particular flight, but was more merely a reflection of the vastly different timescales involved in reaching the nearest stars versus reaching a given Kuiper Belt object. It might well be that similar psychrophile activity had occurred on all of the slowboats which had been sent out across interstellar distances. Marmu-437P knew of six other such launches which had occurred before the departure of this slowboat; it had no way of knowing how many more might have occurred in the following centuries. Moreover, it knew nothing of the fates of those far-flung vessels. Had any reached their destination unscathed? Or had humanity instead merely indulged, in seeking to establish outposts across the middle distance of the solar system's galactic neighbourhood, in an indirect and unintended act of microbial panspermia?

This would become apparent, perhaps, following the ship's arrival at its destination, still some centuries hence. But the appropriate actions to be taken before that event were unclear. Should Marmu-437P arrange a reduction in the storage chambers' temperature, to below the psychrophile's ostensible metabolic threshold? Such an operational change might ensure the problem did not deteriorate further; but to do so would be to place a greater stress on the ship's thermal engineering systems, and an increased risk of catastrophic failure. Should Marmu-437P instead look to revive a small group of the apparently least compromised bodies, especially if within that group there could be identified individuals with expertise of particular value to tackle the psychrophile threat? Yes, that was the appropriate next step. This was a human problem, and it would undoubtedly benefit from a human solution. It would be necessary first to test as widely as possible to determine the individuals with the best prospect for successful revival, and then to maintain those bodies for a sufficient span at a temperature above -80 °C, yet still below freezing, to ensure the psychrophile's full sporulation, and then those bodies could be further warmed to assess their viabil—

τ_5, the protagonist's mission fails. Or: τ_5, a nonhuman opponent triumphs, to an uncertain end. Or: τ_5, the 'fifth element' describing one of the possible widely encountered states of matter, can adequately be defined: absence. Conclude.

Marmu-437P's wheels stopped, and would turn no further. It would be both melodramatic and inaccurate to say that the little mobile unit's lights went out in the same moment, but they may as well have done. For a few decades further the ship monitored the situation silently and with increasing difficulty, and then that activity too ceased. The slowboat drifted on, and the millennia awaited, as the ship's passenger sought to explore the further confines of its new home.

TRILOBITE

Every fossil
a tragedy
every fossil
a reminder

I keep
upon my desk
the death-hunched form
of a trilobite
of black stone
purchased in Canada
in 2003
which as these things go
is only yesterday

A PRELIMINARY REPORT ON THE PRETTY THING

The pretty thing was a pretty thing, we all agreed on that. But we couldn't agree on the rest of it: what it meant, whether it mattered, whether there was any intrinsic value to a pretty thing which served no purpose, whether being a pretty thing was itself some kind of purpose.

It was a woman, some had said, who'd made the pretty thing, or who'd found it, or had acquired it: nobody was sure which, which is to say that some claimed certainty but could not agree with the others' claims. There'd been a woman, then there was the pretty thing, then the woman died or disappeared or some such. Those details weren't connected, or at least there were no broadly accepted claims of connection, but this sequence gave the pretty thing a resonance which it might otherwise have lacked; in the minds of some people, the pretty thing reminded us of the woman, and this was a good thing or a sad thing or an important thing or none of these, depending on who was doing the talking and who was doing the listening, if anyone was, which often they weren't, not really, because those words were heard often, in this place and at that time. But there was the pretty thing, regardless. It was always there, and once you had seen it then you knew it was there, anytime thereafter, whether you were in sight of it or not. That was the way it went, with the pretty thing. Maybe you knew that about it already, but in case you didn't, I've told you now.

The narrative will pause at this point, to allow readers to form an enduring mental image of the pretty thing, which will not be described in any other terms in the text that follows. Some readers won't need that, obviously, but some likely will, and it's the writer's view that a strong mental image of the pretty thing will ensure reader engagement. An opportunity to instil such an image is hereby provided; please make use of it. The writer would suggest that you allow your mind to capture your first idea of the pretty thing's appearance, its form, its characteristics, its properties; this will colour your reaction to the story as it unfolds. You may additionally wish to sketch your own depiction of the pretty thing on this page's margins, but please ensure the book is safely purchased before you commit such an act.

Of course, you maybe know very well what the pretty thing looked like, having seen it, and that will colour your reaction also. Perhaps it has already, because perhaps you know, already, where this is heading.

But enough of that, for the moment.

So there was argument about the pretty thing, and you will know what that was like. Some, who thought the pretty thing worthless, insisted that we should get rid of it; others, who considered it unique and irreplaceable, argued that it must be preserved. Of those decrying its value, there were those who thought disposal should happen in a ceremonious fashion, so all could see that we were not beholden in any way to the pretty thing's attributes; there were others who favoured getting rid of the pretty thing quietly, in case the task were ill-fated in some way, or inconveniently unpopular; some simply did not care whether a fuss was made, or not, when and if the pretty thing was binned. Among those who wanted the pretty thing safeguarded, some held that it should be placed in a vault or other particularly secure and private place, to protect it from those who wished it harm, while others were of the opinion that the pretty thing should remain accessible to everyone, provided we all approached it respectfully and with a supportive attitude. Others who did not hold a strong view in any direction, as regards the pretty thing, could be temporarily swayed towards one preference or another, based on whom they had last spoken with; and always, in the midst of them all, there was the pretty thing, simply existing. What did it mean, that we had this object in our community?

It meant many things, or it would be more accurate to say it was interpreted in many ways. Though the pretty thing was one of a kind, it was of course copied or simulated in various styles and with widely varying degrees of skill and care, by young schoolchildren who were assigned the appearance of the pretty thing as an art project; by older schoolchildren who were asked to describe it in language classes; by senior students who were asked to discuss, in front-of-class presentations and essays and exams, what the pretty thing signified; by artists and sculptors and poets—yes, even poets—who sought to capture the pretty thing's essence in charcoal sketch or watercolour or linocut, marble or bronze, haiku or ode. There were books written about the pretty thing, by academics and chancers, acolytes and sceptics; there were speeches written, and songs, and plays. There was a ballet, or maybe it was an opera. Did any of these attempts truly convey what made the pretty thing special? Few would say that they did, although some liked the songs and some liked the books and some of the paintings and sculptures sold, mainly to visitors who, it must be presumed, wished for something by which to remember their pilgrimage, if that's what it was, to see the pretty thing for themselves. Those of us who lived in the community could see the pretty thing whenever we wanted; we didn't need replicas of it, and probably we didn't trust them.

The ballet, unless it was an opera, was likely only performed once, and few people confessed to having seen it. I never met anyone who had, nor anyone who knew anyone who had. But I knew some who claimed to know someone who knew of an audience member, or of someone who knew one.

It seems scarcely plausible that the simple fact of the pretty thing's existence was sufficient to explain the mystique which, over time, it came to accrue. And yet what else could account for it? The pretty thing did nothing, had never done anything. This didn't stop blame being heaped upon it, when things went poorly, any more than any propitious event occurring in the community might be said by some people to have some mysterious connection to the pretty thing's benevolent qualities, whatever those were. And so it went until the next turning of fate, and the next. And the next.

Some considered the pretty thing offensive, though it was difficult for most of us to see why anyone would believe this. Some called it evil, or cursed, or forbidden, whatever those words actually mean. Some maintained that the pretty thing was repugnant. Others venerated it. There were fights, on occasion, between some of the people referenced in this paragraph, mostly because they were on opposite 'sides' but sometimes because they were on the same 'side' and did not realise it. There were arguments, too, of course, but arguments solve even fewer things than fights, or maybe it's just that they are less fun to watch. I wouldn't know, I've never felt drawn to either. People are strange, and the pretty thing didn't change any of that, unless it focussed it somehow, which again I wouldn't know. And in the wake of the fights, and the arguments, and the arguments which turned into fights and vice versa, some would suggest that the lesson emerging from all this was that the pretty thing was important, while others stated instead that the only conclusion which could be drawn was that the pretty thing was dangerous. So these people too, on occasion, fought, while also insisting that their fights were somehow a higher-minded thing than the brawling of the society's plebeian elements on the exact same subject. You will likely know what that was like too.

You'll have your own views on this, I imagine, tempered perhaps by your own memory of the pretty thing, or otherwise by the mental image evoked by the activity encouraged in the third paragraph. (If you haven't yet formed such a mental image, please do so now, at this point in the third-to-last paragraph: there is still time.)

People saw different things when they gazed at the pretty thing; as with all else described above, this is human nature. And they said different things, and felt different things, and came to blows, sometimes, when they realised that the things they saw or felt or said were too different in some respect from what someone else saw or felt, or said that they saw or felt. It's a wonder, really, that the pretty thing lasted as long as it did, and perhaps it owed its endurance to the legacy of the woman who'd been associated with its origin in some manner, though few now could remember anything substantial about her, assuming there even was any substance to that part of the pretty thing's origin story, which perhaps there was. There was a vague sense that she must have been someone special, which perhaps she was. If she'd existed, which perhaps she had, and which perhaps she still did somewhere. It helped, too, that the thing was pretty: who would wish to destroy such an item? And yet some did.

We've come, now, to the final act in the pretty thing's story: its destruction. But I won't describe that here; you'll know how it goes, and you'll know what happens next.

LIMINAL

It's like water-glass, I suggest to her, not properly knowing what water-glass is, nor what it is I'm comparing it to. To be honest, I didn't hear what she'd said anyway, against the railway station's turmoil. Truth be told, she's not even here, waiting on this bustling platform alongside the other absent people; truth be told, I'm not here either. All that's here are these words on paper, just shapes in ink, and whatever life they hold happens only in your mind, at this moment of reading. You should be careful with that, it can cause a lot of trouble.

ABOUT THE AUTHOR

Born and raised in North Canterbury, New Zealand, Simon Petrie now lives in Canberra, Australia, where he is paid to be careful with words. He has been shortlisted several times for the Sir Julius Vogel, Ditmar, and Aurealis Awards, and has won the Sir Julius Vogel Award three times: in 2010 for Best New Talent and in 2013 and 2018, with *Flight 404* and *Matters Arising from the Identification of the Body* respectively, for Best Novella. He also scored a coveted Dishonourable Mention in the 2011 Bulwer-Lytton Fiction Contest.

He has edited five issues (numbers 35, 40, 51, 54, and 61) of *Andromeda Spaceways Inflight Magazine*, and has co-edited two anthologies (*Light Touch Paper, Stand Clear* and *Use Only As Directed*) with Edwina Harvey and one (*Next*) with Rob Porteous.

A reformed academic, Simon's publishing history also includes numerous studies on the upper-atmosphere chemistry of the Saturnian moon Titan; on the ion/molecule chemistry of the dense interstellar cloud TMC-1 and the circumstellar envelope of the post-asymptotic-giant-branch star IRC+10216; on the gas-phase chemistry of multiply-charged fullerene ions; and on the structure of the active site of the water-oxidising complex within Photosystem II. He holds actionable views about second person present tense, em-dashes, and Oxford commas.

ACKNOWLEDGEMENTS

Several of the stories included herein have been previously published. 'Optimal' first aired in *Banksia Journal* (ed. Brittany Lee) in February 2005. 'Living room' was first published in issue 42 of *Brilliant Flash Fiction* (ed. Dawn Lowe) in June 2024. 'Of why the sea', edited by Claire Corbett, first appeared in *Overland*'s Friday Fiction category in February 2024. 'Steer' was first published in the March 2025 issue of *Crepuscular Magazine* (ed. Rebecca Treasure). 'Pruning shears' was published in issue 49 of *The Colored Lens* (ed. Dawn Lloyd), in October 2023. 'Carbon copy', edited by Agatha Grimke, aired in issue 2 of *In Another Time*, in June 2024. 'The first ten multiples of 18' was initially published as a series of tweets on my now-defunct Twitter account on 17 November 2022. 'Better than one' was published in the July 2025 issue of *Antipodean SF* (issue 321), edited by Ion Newcombe. 'Liminal', edited by D W White, appeared in issue X of *L'Esprit Literary Review*, in February 2025.

Excepting 'Hexagonal' and 'Trilobite', two short poems on which I reckon I can be marginally trusted, all the other items in the collection have been edited by the indomitable James Morrison, who is also to be fulsomely thanked for the gorgeous cover image.

ALSO BY THIS AUTHOR

80,000 Totally Secure Passwords That No Hacker Would Ever Guess

A varied and misleadingly titled collection of short stories.

Paperback: 978-0-6483228-6-3

Ebook: 978-0-6483228-7-0

The 1001 Top Immortality Treatments You Must Try Before You Die

A varied and misleadingly titled collection of other short stories.

Paperback: 978-0-6483836-3-5

Ebook: 978-0-6483836-4-2

Murder On The Zenith Express (the Gordon Mamon collection)

The (now no longer quite complete) adventures of space-hotel employee and reluctant sleuth Gordon Mamon.

Paperback: 978-0-6483228-8-7

Ebook: 978-0-6483228-9-4

Tremendously Inconveniencing A Great Many Photons

An uplifting short novel about pottos, First Contact, and interstellar spaceflight.

Paperback: 978-0-6483836-1-1

Ebook: 978-0-6483836-2-8

Flight 404

The search for the *Bougainvillaea* brings investigator Charmaine Mertz back to the unwelcoming world of her boyhood.

(Winner of the 2013 Sir Julius Vogel award for Best Novella.)

Paperback: 978-0-6483228-4-9
Ebook: 978-0-6483228-5-6

Matters Arising From The Identification Of The Body

Tanja Morgenstein, daughter of a wealthy industrialist and a geochemist, is dead from exposure to Titan's lethal, chilled atmosphere, and Guerline Scarfe must determine why.

(Winner of the 2018 Sir Julius Vogel award for Best Novella.)

Paperback: 978-0-6483228-0-1
Ebook: 978-0-6483228-1-8

Wide Brown Land (stories of Titan)

A collection of eleven hard-SF short stories set on the Solar System's most intriguing moon.

Paperback: 978-0-6483228-2-5
Ebook: 978-0-6483228-3-2

Soft Dim Skies (a story of Titan)

It's important to Cory that his past misdeeds aren't uncovered. It's important to Portia that her mentor's death hasn't been in vain. A novella, connecting several threads begun in *Wide Brown Land*.

Paperback: 978-0-6483836-5-9
Ebook: 978-0-6483836-6-6

Wayfaring Stranger

Aboard the airship *Wayfaring Stranger*, researcher Solveig Robertson struggles to find a place alongside her colleagues and amidst the varied upper-atmosphere lifeforms of the planet Rousseau.

Paperback only: 978-0-6483836-7-3